ONCE MORE ROUND THE SUN

A Year of Dark Stories

DAVE MUSSON

ONCE MORE ROUND
THE SUN

"Musson is an obvious student of the craft, and has applied all he's learned to create a collection so compelling that you won't be able to put it down, despite finding yourself terrified at times!"
Jason Pellegrini, author of *The Replacement*

"Genuinely unsettling weird Albion folk horror delivered with a fiendish twinkle in the eye"
Garth Jones, author of *Home Brewed, Vampire Bullets*

"In a flurry of stories, Musson manages to mix beauty with brutality, love with lust, heartfelt connection with horrific catastrophe, and gentleness with gore. Stephen King would blush to know the dark creativity his writing has inspired. Horror lovers, take notice, *Once More Round the Sun* is a collection that should not be slept on... and it just might keep you turning the pages well after bedtime."
Thomas Gloom, author of the *Stories With Horror & Heart* **series**

"Musson has the enviable talent of luring readers into his stories with only a few words. He gets the reader to invest then delivers a devastating emotional blow that should be criminal. Sometimes that blow isn't always down to the horror of the situation. Take *You're Melting* for example, a tender story about love lost. Yes, there's horror here, but you can't help but feel touched as well as repulsed. As a collection I feel that Musson is toying with his readers in each story. Each one seems to pick one of the five senses to invoke tension and dread. In *Anchor*, where the protagonist is confined to a hospital bed with the drapes closed. Musson assaults the reader with the protagonist hyper sensitivity to the noises around him. It's a small thing, yet it creates such emotions that it highlights how much Musson can do with the smallest of things."

Jamie Stewart, author of *Montague's Carnival of Delights and Terror*

CONTENTS

For Reuben & Aubrey

Start As You Mean
To Go On

A slight breeze crept through the bedroom window, which was on vent as usual, and he stirred. He was awake, but kept his eyes shut while he savoured the feeling of not just a new day, but a whole new *year*.

He smiled. 2024. *2024!* A year that still sounded all kinds of futuristic to him, despite him waking up in it, right here and now. It just didn't seem possible that he could be living in such a sci-fi sounding year. It was eight years after *Back to the Future Part II*, for God's sake!

He chuckled to himself.

Despite what he'd spent the last few weeks telling anyone who asked–that New Year is a load of bollocks and doesn't change how you feel about yourself or, well, *anything*–it seemed he was wrong.

He felt good. He felt great, in fact. But, most of all, he felt *different*.

The thing was, though, he couldn't work out *what* was different. Perhaps it was just, after more than three years of lockdown, pandemic, and general fucking misery caused by living in a country governed by cruel, self-serving vampires, this year felt like a chance to get moving again, to be normal again.

To *live* again.

He relented and opened his eyes. Perhaps waking up another sense would help him to pin it down. He stared at his bedroom ceiling, taking in the three large cracks in the plaster, the stain left behind from the leak last summer that his landlord had *still* not properly fixed, and the intricate collection of spider webs that hung off each prong of the ornate, but awful light.

He was still smiling, but not moving—just lying on his back in the middle of the bed, legs spread out away from his body and both arms flung out behind and to the side, tucked under his pillows. There was a strange tingling on his right buttock that he couldn't quite place, but it was probably just pins and needles—he always was a heavy sleeper after drinking, and often woke with dead limbs after big nights out.

He closed his eyes and tried to get back on track. Now...what was it? What was different?

For a moment, a few images flashed up from the night before: drinks, his friends, dancing, more drinks, more dancing, more drinks, more fun!

But nothing substantial came to mind. He tried to let his grey matter float and ponder it further, but was quickly distracted by the sounds and smells of breakfast being made downstairs. Something was sizzling in the frying pan—bacon, if what his nose was shouting at him was anything to go by—and coffee being brewed too.

A fine start to 2024!

Yet still, that feeling of *different*. It wouldn't go away. If anything, it was starting to bug him.

As far as he could remember—which, admittedly, was not very far—nothing unusual had happened last night. As it turned out, it was pretty quiet for a New Year's Eve. Spending a couple of recent ones in lockdown had really shown him both how overhyped the whole thing was, as well as—weirdly—how he missed the normality that the annual let-down of going out on the 31st of December brought with it. He'd had a few drinks, sure, and he had no recollection of seeing his friends beyond about 11 p.m., but nothing bigger than that. The club had been busy, probably because it was the only one in Kingsworth, all the other places that were still open at midnight were curry houses and takeaway joints. Everyone in the club wanted to dance, to hug, to feel normal. It was no big deal.

So...why this new feeling? It wasn't just the tingling, almost stinging, of his buttock. How was it that the switch from one year to the next had left him feeling so different?

He wiggled his toes, enjoying the feeling of those rough digits tickling the underside of the duvet cover that he'd pushed down below his knees at some point during the night. He noticed the slight scratching sound made by his toenails on that bunched up cover too. His ex had hated that sound—*hated* it—to the point where he'd become cripplingly self-conscious about it and often lay awake for hours in desperately uncomfortable positions but unable to move for fear of his toes accidentally scratching the covers and waking her up. But now, with her long gone and this brand new year to savour, he found his toenails played a rather pleasant tune.

He let them play on a little longer.

The sizzling downstairs had stopped. He heard some clunking around: drawers being opened, things being removed—metal things and ceramic things too—drawers being shut again, then footsteps climbing the stairs slowly.

Think now, he told himself, *what am I missing here?*

He remembered the countdown to midnight, remembered the balloon drop, remembered singing *Auld Lang Syne* arm-in-arm with a stranger either side and beaming from ear-to-ear. But after that, little else. As his brain had already registered, he'd lost his friends long before the big countdown, but that same brain reminded him that on New Year's Eve things like that simply didn't matter.

What is it?

His buttock was still making itself known—the pins and needles feeling was almost painful now—so he tried to flex his calf on that side to loosen everything up a bit more. Christ, it was tight.

I should make daily stretching my first resolution, he thought and revelled in that feeling again. The sensation eased a little, but nowhere near as much as he'd hoped. It was getting uncomfortable.

The footsteps were now about halfway up the stairs, each tread accompanied by the rattle of metal and porcelain on a tray.

More images flashed into his mind from last night; the lights coming on, waiting in line for the cloakroom with someone else's hand in his, the cold December—no, *January*—air on his face biting at his cheeks, a pair of beautiful eyes, a perfect smile, full lips, and a lingering goodnight kiss.

Perhaps I was just wrong after all, he admitted to himself, still lying in that same cosy, sunk-so-far-into-the-mattress-it-seems-criminal-to-move position from earlier, despite the stinging—yep, definitely stinging—feeling from his still-asleep rump. *Maybe this is my New Year's light bulb moment. Maybe New Year's is good.*

With that thought, he was suddenly filled with the excitement of possibility. He was eager to tackle this new lap of the sun head on. He wanted to make this new year, this 2024, *his*.

As the footsteps carrying his breakfast reached

the top of the stairs and turned onto the landing, he finally decided to make a start on his year and set about actually moving. After all, you can't change the world from just lying in bed—not even John and Yoko managed it.

At first, he couldn't either. He couldn't do anything.

He couldn't move.

Wow, he thought. *I did sleep well.*

He tried again, and still found himself virtually paralysed. It was almost as if his arms and legs were held in place, which was weird—this sheer level of post-sleep grogginess was definitely some-thing new. Even his chest felt tight and heavy, like it was still asleep or under a weighted blanket—something like that, anyway. For the first time this morning—this year—his smile faltered. His fore-head grew clammy and his now positively-painful buttock still hadn't woken up.

Those footsteps were almost at the bedroom door now, still with the rattle of various unseen items and utensils accompanying each step. He tried again, wanting to receive his first breakfast of the new year sitting up and bright-eyed, but couldn't do it.

That was the moment it hit him. *Now* he knew what was different. He couldn't believe it had taken him this long. In fact, it was right there in front of him, blindly obvious.

And horrifying.

He lived alone.

Or, at least, he *had* lived alone until last night. He wasn't alone anymore.

He finally shifted his gaze and took a proper look at himself. His arms and legs had felt like they were being held in place because, well, they *were* being held in place, by shackles and chains. His chest felt weighed down because it *was* weighed down, with thick leather straps cinched across it. Then his eyes saw the red under his buttock and his brain finally sensed the wetness there and he realised two things: that it wasn't pins and needles he was feeling, and that it hadn't been bacon he'd smelled cooking downstairs.

His heartbeat rocketed as the bedroom door creaked open. A figure, wearing nothing more than a thin silk kimono that was loosely tied at the waist and carrying a tray with a whole host of delights on it, appeared. Some of those delights were baked, some fried, some brewed.

The rest of them were sharp. Very sharp.

That figure carrying the tray had beautiful eyes, a perfect smile, and full lips. She was stunning, she was incredible...she was terrifying.

His instinct was to scrabble backwards, but he barely moved an inch before all the strong, locked things holding him in place brought him to an abrupt and painful stop. He looked at the figure in the doorway again. This time he saw beyond the eye-catching beauty. He saw what hid under its mask.

While her face *was* unbelievably beautiful, and her figure was the petite and curvy kind that normally sent him wild, there was something off. Underneath that thin, sham outer layer of glamour something was moving, *slithering*, and desperate to get out. She noticed him looking and her smile grew wider. Still, whatever it was beneath her skin was rippling faster. She was excited, and he was all the more scared for it.

Gripping her tray in her left hand, with her right, she slowly untied her dressing gown without losing eye contact with her bound bedmate. With an effortless shimmy, the silky garment floated to the floor revealing her full form, which had stopped pulsing and had switched back to being an object of desire; full, pale breasts, a soft, flat stomach, a perfect triangle of dark pubic hair just above two smooth, toned thighs.

He stared at her, unable to look away, and felt himself becoming aroused.

She noticed, and her eyes glowed silver. She took in a deep, exaggerated breath—arching her head to ensure her chest rose slowly. Then she cocked her right knee, pressing her toes into the carpet to emphasise her shapely legs. His erection became hard and full. She slowly lowered her eyes to admire this, before locking eyes with him and biting her lower lip. He groaned as every part of him from the waist down throbbed.

He stared back as her teeth kept growing—thin, pointed things that had no right being there—before snapping the fingers on her right hand. In an instant, her perfect skin turned grey, saggy, and scaly. It began to ripple again, this time more frantic and agitated than before. The room was suddenly filled with the smell of rotting meat and spoiled fruit.

In spite of his fear, he ejaculated with a gasp. The figure's pulsing body rippled with delight and her hideous mouth slowly pushed itself into a wide, awful smile—the tendons in her neck creaking as it continued to push out further and further.

"Happy New Year!" she said, and slowly walked towards the bed.

The Strange Phenomenon of Epping Manor

BBC News online article, dated Saturday, 17 February, 10:18 a.m.

Fears grow for missing supernatural podcaster

Family and friends of the podcaster Felix Devine have spoken of their growing concern for the broadcaster's whereabouts.

Thirty-two-year-old Devine—whose legal name is Frederic Davidson—was last seen in Kingsworth, Warwickshire, on Tuesday when they were dropped off by an Uber driver at the site of a half-demolished mansion. They were there to record a new episode of their hit podcast *There Used To Be a House Here*.

In a statement posted via their agent's X, formerly known as Twitter, account today, Devine's mother, Annie, sister, Charlotte, and two friends listed as Sascha and Simeon urged the presenter to make contact with one of them.

The statement said: "We're sick with worry as to the whereabouts of Felix, who hasn't been seen since Tuesday. It is very unlike them not to check in with at least one of us after recording a new episode, and we're now concerned something has happened to them."

It added: "Felix, if you're reading this, please get in touch with us—any of us. If anyone else knows how we can find him, please contact the police. We just want to know they're OK."

There Used To Be a House Here, the podcast created and presented by Devine, explores the legends of houses that no longer stand, and has proved hugely popular in the three years it has existed, drawing in more than a million listeners per episode.

The show's format sees Devine explore the locations of these 'missing' houses, commentating as they walk around and share what they find—often in shocking and scary ways.

Critics have claimed the show is completely fabricated, something Devine has always denied.

When asked for comment, Kingsworth Police confirmed they were actively investigating Devine's disappearance, but did not have any new updates to report.

A spokesperson said: "If anyone has any more information about Mr. Davidson's disappearance, please get in touch as a matter of urgency."

***

Meeting room 4, Kingsworth Police Station, Saturday, 17 February, late morning

Detective Louise Charnley opens the door to the meeting room with her elbow while gripping a lukewarm mug of coffee in one hand and her tablet, laptop, phone, and a cluster of papers in the other. She pulls it off with well-practised ease before flicking the door shut behind her with her foot.

"Solomon,"—she smiles at the pale, bearded officer sitting at the table—"your email could not have been much better timed. I mean, I *knew* you'd be able to recover those, but hearing that you have has been particularly good news today."

Solomon Klein grins back. He's not a police officer—not a Bobby-on-the-beat type member of the team, anyway. But he is a vital part of the police machine, one of the most skilled and sought-after staff in the digital forensics unit—a master of bringing seemingly dead and buried files back to life and into action.

Hell, it's more than that. Solomon is seen by his colleagues as a miracle worker. You could count on one hand the number of people in that building —at all levels—who don't owe Solomon a favour or two.

"The piece on the BBC, right?" he asks and

Louise nods. "I imagine that ruffled some feathers upstairs."

"You bet it has," she says, "and not just because our statement completely ignored Devine's chosen name and pronouns so we come across as a bunch of bigots. The BBC just brings too many eyeballs and too much pressure with it—a week ago, most of the people in the room I've just left didn't even know what a podcast was. Now they can't budge for Felix Devine and their bloody show. And on a flipping Saturday no less."

She takes a swig of coffee and grimaces—too cold. That small window where it was the perfect temperature to drink had slammed shut.

"It is a good show to be fair, even if it is a fake," Solomon says.

Louise admits, "I've never listened. I do *Welcome to Night Vale* and *Heavyweight*—no time for much else."

She sighs and continues. "Anyway, much as I would love to get a bunch of podcast recommendations from you, it'll have to wait. You said you'd managed to open the files?"

Solomon smiles. "Yes, four files have been recovered. I've skimmed through them quickly just to check they're OK, but haven't done a proper listen—I thought you'd want to do that yourself."

"Thanks. You stay while I listen? Just in case of any technical difficulties."

"Sure. Are you ready to push play?"

The only thing connected to Felix Devine that had been found so far since the podcaster went missing earlier that week had been their portable audio recorder—lapel mic still attached. The battery was dead and the SD card inside at first appeared to be corrupted beyond salvation.

But, much to the relief of his colleagues, Solomon had returned from some annual leave this morning and got right to work on it. As always, he'd come up trumps. Louise was eager to hear what had been hiding on that damned card.

"Yes, let's crack on," Louise says, swiping on her tablet. "I'll take notes as it plays."

Solomon nods, turns up the volume on his laptop, and opens the first file.

File name: *VOC_03646_001*

The first sound is the general background ambience of being outside: some birdsong, a gentle breeze, and the sound of a car driving past. Then there's a rustling, a small clunk, and finally a voice.

Check, check.

More background ambience for a moment.

Welcome, welcome, welcome everyone—it's me again, Felix Devine, proud to bring you another episode of *There Used To Be a House Here*, the show that puts the 'odd' in podcast. Don't forget to follow the show on Instagram—@used2bahouse—and check out our Patreon for all kinds of behind-the-scenes available to you if you sign up. Our regular feed lets you peep through the keyhole —our Patreons get to stay the night!

This episode, I'm—

Felix's voice is drowned out by a large vehicle—a lorry or possibly something more agricultural, like a tractor—rumbling past. It passes, eventually.

Fucking farmers. These edits take long enough to sort without that sort of shit on top. A tractor! Honestly!

A brief pause.

This episode, I'm in rural Warwickshire to investigate the strange phenomenon of Epping Manor. This place was once the jewel in the crown of the town of Kingsworth, before becoming plagued with scandal and mystery and eventually being abandoned decades ago.

The local council began to demolish the place in 2017, before a series of budget cuts, other projects, and then COVID left the job half-finished. However, the wrecking ball is due before the end of the month, meaning it's now or never for me to take you for a look around. So, let's go.

The sound of footsteps on tarmac can be heard, while the occasional bursts of traffic noise gradually get quieter.

I'm just walking down the main drive to Epping Manor. The gate has been boarded off, but the Council kindly gave me permission to enter and have entrusted me with the access code—I just hope I've not lost the piece of paper they wrote it on.

The footsteps stop. There is the sound of general rummaging in pockets, before a whispered 'yes' and then paper being unfolded.

Eight-six-three-two—bingo!

The sound of a door opening.

Shit, mental note to edit that bit out.

The sound of a door closing.

OK, the drive continues ahead of me for a

few hundred metres, then bends off to the left. I assume the remains of the Manor will be round that way. Looks like I have time to give you the essential background while I walk to the house.

The footsteps begin again.

So, Epping Manor was built in 1828, by one Jacob Epping, Kingsworth's most famous businessman who made his money from wool, and made a lot of it. The Manor was a wedding present for his son Joshua and new daughter-in-law Marie.

The footsteps are now in a steady rhythm. There's still the occasional birdsong, but little else.

For the first hundred years, the Manor was everything Jacob had hoped: lavish, beautiful, and the centre of the Kingsworth social scene. Its parties were legendary for no reason other than being good, wholesome events. Over that century, four generations of Eppings lived and grew up there, and kept the house ticking over. The Eppings were all men—all their kids were boys who grew into men. Just normal, innocent, *boring* men.

Needless to say that, so far as this podcast goes, nothing interesting happened in that time.

More walking.

But things started changing in 1929. Edith

Epping—the first Epping girl to be born here and Jacob's great-granddaughter of either five or six jumps; I can't remember off the top of my head—went missing in the grounds and was never found. One minute, she'd been playing with her doll outside; the next, she had vanished. They found the doll, but not her.

That seemed to bring a curse on the house, and the next thirty years or so saw it become a place locals feared. Between 1929 and 1962, nineteen different children disappeared on the grounds of the Manor, along with seven dogs and twelve adults, all of them doing nothing more sinister than visiting the latest line of the Epping clan to live in the Manor. Friends, family, even a postman. All gone—POOF!

The house had earned itself an unwanted reputation over those years as a haunted place, and the Eppings had to employ security to keep fans of the supernatural from breaking in. Naturally, the parties and social gatherings had long-since stopped.

More footsteps.

Anyway, the killer blow was in 1976, when the Dominion Cult found a way to beat security. If you listen to this podcast regularly, you'll know about Dominion—fucking lunatics with branches all over the country, each one specialising in a different nutjob mission.

'Round here, the Dominion freaks claimed that the only way to solve the Epping Manor conundrum was a blood sacrifice, so they scaled the walls, snuck through to the lawn, and slit their own throats—all fifty-seven of them.

Unsurprisingly, the Eppings didn't feel comfortable sticking around after that, so they cut their losses and moved elsewhere. The Council actually purchased the property from them as no one else would touch it. Every so often, something—some kind of use of the place—would get suggested in meetings—a community centre, a writers' retreat, a health space—but those ideas never got worked up and the Manor started to rot.

The footsteps stop.

And, speaking of the Manor, I can see what's left of it.

The walking starts again, but slower.

Well, the wrecking ball won't have much to do here; there really isn't a lot still standing, although what is here does show what a grand place this once must have been—the detail surrounding the windows is excellent. There's also a spectacular stone archway between the house and the garden that the Council really should try and save—it's beautiful.

Felix stops.

Wait. Wait a second.

Their breathing quickens.

I can see something! God, I didn't think things would happen this quickly. Something behind one of those windows, on the third floor. It's seen me. It's staring right at me. Shit, what should I do? I'm completely exposed here.

It's opening the window. It's ... it's ...it's ...

It's a quick word from our sponsor.

The recording clicks off.

Meeting room 4, Kingsworth Police Station

"Do they do that every episode?" Louise asks, unable to hide the unimpressed tone from her voice.

"They used to," Solomon replies. "They've not done it for over a year though. They must have been bored."

Solomon's finger glides across the trackpad as he closes one file and readies another.

"Please don't take this as a swipe in your direction, Solomon," Louise says, "because the fact we now have *anything* from that memory card is your latest technical miracle. But—"

"But the other files had better have something that is actually fucking useful, right?" Solomon cuts in.

Louise laughs. It's a tired laugh, but a real one. "You got it!"

Solomon chuckles and takes a swig from the bright orange water bottle he always has with him.

"So," he starts, "that was file 001. The next one I found on there is 008—I've hunted for anything that might have accounted for the bits in between, pushed it through all my best toys, and have found nothing. I left something running—a final try—while I came to show you what we do have, but I'm not hopeful of anything coming up. And there are gaps in the numbers between the others too."

"OK," Louise replies while squinting her eyes shut and massaging the top of her nose with her finger and thumb. "We'll worry about that more if we need to. What's important is that we do have something. Let's push on."

"Right you are," says Solomon, and double clicks.

The now-familiar voice of Felix Devine starts out of his laptop speakers only for Louise's phone to loudly wail into life almost immediately. She swipes the screen and holds it to her ear, mouthing 'sorry' at Solomon as she does.

"Charnley," she snaps, then listens.

Solomon goes to stop the file, when he hears it.

Solomon, whispered in a child's voice.

He frowns at his laptop speaker, momentarily flabbergasted.

"We're in room 4."

He becomes aware of Louise speaking and quickly pauses the audio file, hoping she hasn't noticed him turning red with embarrassment.

"We're listening to them now. One down, three to go."

There is a moment where no one makes a sound.

"Yeah, you can join us," Louise says, then mouths 'Paul'—the name of her partner on this case—to Solomon, who gives a thumbs up in return. "We'll hold fire until you get here. Can you bring fresh coffees? Thanks."

Louise hangs up.

"I'm going to pop to the bathroom; be right back," she says, and leaves before Solomon can respond.

His focus is entirely on the audio file. The file that he swears just whispered his name. He uses his finger to pull the cursor back a few seconds and then pushes play again.

Nothing—just the sound of crunching footsteps and that general outdoorsy background noise for a few seconds before Felix's voice starts up again.

Solomon pushes pause again, takes the cursor back to where it was when Louise's phone rang, then sighs.

Just my imagination, he thinks, and takes the opportunity to check his emails.

After dumping a few things into the trash and flagging one to follow up later, Solomon pauses and gives in to the nagging thought that has been pinging around his brain all morning—ever since he saw what he was going to be working on. Not Felix or the podcast, but the house.

Epping Manor.

Felix was broadly accurate in their history of

the place when they said no one wanted to buy it. But, in one hell of a coincidence, there *had* been one potential buyer: Solomon's father.

Late 1981, it had been. The Manor had been vacant for around five years but was still in decent condition, and Solomon's parents had fled the big city for a quiet spell in the country. They had money, and the Manor was priced to sell. Solomon has heard the story of his father showing his pregnant wife around, liking it, but ultimately settling for a mid-century property on the other side of town countless times.

Solomon had been born a few months later. Learning of the Manor's history growing up, he'd always wondered *what if*. That place was nearly his home; it was close to maybe being known as the Klein House.

It could have been home, Solomon ponders. *What might* that *have been like?*

The daydream is interrupted with a jolt as he hears the distinctive booming voice of Detective Paul Bowers, along with Louise's laughter in return—both getting closer to the meeting room door, which had been left ajar.

Solomon fixes his face and looks up as his colleagues reach the door.

Solomon. Solomon. Come.

Solomon's mouth goes dry. He swears he hears that child whispering his name again, coming out of the laptop speakers even though no audio files are playing, but then Paul and Louise are barrelling in and he can't do anything about it.

Paul grins without humour. He's one of those rare folk whose appearance matches his voice; both are big, full, commanding. He also has the precise beard, haircut, and collection of creases around his eyes and across his forehead that you'd expect just from hearing him speak.

"Alright, Solomon?" he asks, setting down two mugs of coffee on the table. "Good holiday?"

"Great thanks, Paul," Solomon replies, taking one of the mugs, "and cheers for this! Appreciate it."

"No problem, mate." Paul still has the remains of a Cockney twang to his accent despite having tried really hard to lose it since moving to the Midlands. He doesn't like how it marks him as an outsider. He hears it now and readjusts.

"Lou tells me I've not missed anything with the first file; let's see if the second one is different."

By now, Louise has taken her seat again and is ready with her tablet open on the notes app.

Solomon touches the trackpad again.

"OK," he says, "here we go."

File name: VOC_03646_008

Over the sound of the same outdoor ambience of the previous file is some heavy breathing. It is Felix; they sound like they've been running.

I'm not entirely sure what's happening here.

More heavy breathing.

I've only been here forty minutes. It's early afternoon in February, and yet it's getting dark on these grounds. I don't see how it's possible. I'm heading to some trees just away from the remains of the house—I feel too exposed here.

Footsteps, but much quicker than they were in the first file. They soon stop and are followed by more heavy breathing.

OK. That feels a little better. Being over by the house ... I swear someone was watching me. I know you'll all think I'm taking the piss because of the ad break fake jump scare I did earlier, but this is for real.

More breathing.

It was creepy. And not just from one place. It felt like I was being watched from all sides. From far away, but from nearby too.

After this is around fifty seconds of just outdoor ambience. Then, a whisper.

Solomon. Come home.

Meeting room 4, Kingsworth Police Station

Solomon looks up at his colleagues, trying not to show how scared he is and is thankful that they can't see the trickle of sweat running down his back.

They must *have heard that*, he thinks.

But if they did, they're showing no sign. Paul glances up, smiles at Solomon, then stares at the speaker again as if to better focus his attention.

Solomon tries to do the same.

File name: VOC_03646_008, continued

The noise of someone sighing is picked up, then more talking.

Wait. It's getting light again. What the fuck is going on with this pla—

A pause.

What the hell is that?

Another pause. Then—quiet at first—the sound of children laughing. It gets louder, presumably getting closer to Felix's recorder.

Fuck this!

The sound of running comes at the same time that the sound of the children laughing fades away. The running eventually stops and there is more heavy breathing.

OK ... I ... I ... honestly don't know what to do next.

More heavy breathing. Then a loud crack—like a branch being snapped—is heard, followed by a sharp, surprised intake of breath.

Shit!

There is a loud thud, then the file stops.

Meeting room 4, Kingsworth Police Station

Solomon, Louise, and Paul are all fully enraptured by the laptop speakers now. Their coffees are all only half-drunk and will remain that way until the office cleaners come in that evening.

No one knows what to say for a few moments.

"How many more files did you recover?" asks Paul eventually.

"Two more," Solomon confirms, then says it again for no other reason than to break the monumental silence that has invaded the room. "Two more."

Another empty space fills the stuffy and now somewhat-claustrophobic meeting room.

"Well," Louise at last whispers, for no other reason than whispering feels appropriate, "let's see what's on the next one."

"Sure," Solomon whispers back and double clicks as gently as he can, not daring to cause unnecessary noise.

File name: VOC_03646_011

A SCREECHING, AWFUL, HORRENDOUS WHITE NOISE POURS OUT OF THE LAPTOP

SPEAKERS AND FILLS THE AIR OF THE MEETING ROOM. IT'S THE AUDIO EQUIV-ALENT OF A VISE GRIP AROUND THE TEM-PLES WHILE ALSO BEING REPEATEDLY STABBED IN THE FACE WITH SEWING NEEDLES. IT'S ONLY PLAYED FOR THREE SECONDS BUT IS SO PAINFUL, SO AWFUL, IT FEELS LIKE HOURS.

Meeting room 4, Kingsworth Police Station

Solomon slams the space bar and the audio pauses. Both Louise and Paul are grimacing.

"God, sorry. I skimmed through all these files before coming here, and none of them did that. It's so weird."

"Is the whole file like that?" asks Louise.

"Let me check," says Solomon.

"Can you do it without pushing play?" Paul asks, "I don't think my ears can take any more of that."

"Yes, give me a sec." Solomon clicks a few times then turns his screen to show his colleagues a soundwave. "So," he says, pointing at the screen, "it looks like the whole file is loud, white noise apart from this section ... here."

He points to the only part of the soundwave that isn't a solid white, angry block.

"Let's see what happened there." Solomon moves across the trackpad, clicks once, then hovers his finger over the space bar again. He looks up.

Paul nods. So does Louise.

Solomon lets his finger drop.

File name: VOC_03646_011

The familiar mixture of heavy breathing over that general outdoor background ambience is there again. Then, the same word repeated three times by Felix.

No ... no! ... NO!

Then the white noise returns at crippling volume.

Meeting room 4, Kingsworth Police Station

Everyone in the room is breathing too quickly, their eyes too wide.

"One more file, is it?" asks Paul.

"Yep. Just let me just check the wave before I push play."

As Solomon does some clicking, Louise takes a swig of coffee and grimaces. Too cold—again.

"It generally looks OK," says Solomon without moving his eyes up from his screen. "There are some patches of it, but they're only a few seconds long each, apart from a big one at the end. I've just reduced the volume on those bits, so our ears should be OK."

He pushes play for the final time.

File name: VOC_03646_013

It's just got dark for the third time since I've been here, and now it's light again. I don't get it. It's as though this place has its own time zone or something.

Heavy breathing.

OK, I think I need to leave ... I don't see what else I can achieve by being here other than scaring myself shitless, so I'm going to head back down the drive. I just need to go past the house one more time.

Footsteps. Tentative this time. Then a sudden stop. Shit.

Felix is whispering again.

Shit, shit, shit. There's someone up ahead. In the archway. I can't see who, just a silhouette. I can't even tell if they're facing me, but I'm not sticking here to find out. I'm going the long way round.

WHITE NOISE.

What the fu—

WHITE NOISE.

OK, I'm round the back of the house, away from the archway and whoever was standing in it. They don't seem to have followed me. It's fully daylight again and I think I can see where I need to go.

Footsteps.

What the—? That is … weird.

The footsteps stop.

So, up ahead is a perfectly straight row of trees. There are … um … uh … one, two … six … eleven … uh … nineteen of them. It looks like there's a small plaque in front of each. I *swear* these weren't here earlier. In fact, I'm certain—I'll have my description from earlier on one of the other files that'll confirm it.

A pause.

Wait, that's creepy. Nineteen trees, nineteen

kids who went missing here over time. That seems like too deliberate to be a coinci—

WHITE NOISE.

Heavy breathing. Felix continues to whisper.

It's full dark again, except for over the trees. The trees are fully lit up as if there's spotlights on them or something, and everything else is dark. What the hell—

WHITE NOISE.

The leaves are falling from the trees. One at a time at first, but now it's like it's snowing—they're going to be bare in a few seconds. I've never seen anything like this; they all just ... let go ... together, like they're falling in slow motion—huh?

A pause.

The trees are in darkness. Everything is dark, even though it is about two in the afternoon in mid-February. What the hell is—OH GOD!

A pause.

Jesus Christ.

Another pause.

What the actual fuck?! Oh ... oh, SHIT!

The sound of retching and sobbing.

It's fully daylight again and from every tree I

can now see a child hanging. I don't understand what is ...

A crack.

Shit! They all just looked up at me. Fuck this.

Running. Panting. More running.

WHITE NOISE

Still running.

I've found the drive. I'm ... getting ... the ... hell ... out of here.

Shoes thudding on the tarmac.

WHITE NOISE

No. No! It can't be dark again!

More running.

WHITE NOISE

The running tapers off to a stop.

What?

Heavy breathing.

That can't be ... I never left the path or changed direction. I ... that's not possible. I've been running for at least fifteen minutes.

Silence, apart from that outdoor background ambience from earlier.

How can I be back at the house?

A few hesitant steps.

What the—?

The sound of children laughing again, only this time, it's getting much louder, much faster than before. It slowly becomes clear that, actually, they're not laughing. They're yelling, wailing ... screaming. And it's not just children screaming. There are adult voices in there, too, as well as the sound of—not footsteps—but something, many somethings, shuffling over the ground.

No. NO! Fuck off! FUCK OFF!

Heavy, panicked breathing.

NO! YOU CAN'T! NO! HELP! HEEEELLLPPPP—

WHITE NOISE FOR THE REMAINING SIX MINUTES OF THE FILE.

Meeting room 4, Kingsworth Police Station

All three people look at each other with wide eyes. No one says anything for a moment.

"That's everything," Solomon says after a while. "I ... I don't know if that's helped or not."

Paul runs his fingers through his hair, but says nothing.

Louise lets out a huge sigh. "It does. Solomon. At the very least, we know to focus the search around the house remains, and we should try and find that line of trees."

She utters a single, humourless grunt of a laugh.

"I mean, we *won't* find it—not a chance in hell because it isn't there—but we should try."

She stands up. "Come on, Paul. We need to move," she says to her partner.

Paul also stands.

"Right, yes," he says shakily. "Let's do it. Thanks, Solomon."

The two detectives leave the room, and Solomon takes another long swig of water before closing his laptop. He pushes his chair back from the table, then turns away from the door to crouch down and unplug his machine—he hadn't dared relying on battery power for such an important playback.

So much whizzes through his head he almost can't bear it: Felix, the national interest in his little town and place of work, those sounds, the weirdly corrupted files, and, of course, the house that in another where and another when might have been his home.

Solomon.

His name, whispered by a child again. But not from his laptop this time.

Solomon. Come home!

Whispered again, but this time from a bunch of children. And definitely not from his laptop.

Solomon!

It's coming from …

Come home!

Directly …

Come home, please!

Behind him.

Solomon slowly stands up, keeping his back to the door and telling himself it's all in his head. Then the lights go out and the voice speaks again, only this time not in a whisper. It's very loud and very close. The invisible breath from the invisible mouths powering it tickles the nape of Solomon's neck. Then they stop only to be replaced by a different speaker.

"Solomon, come home," says the voice of Felix Devine from the corner of the darkened meeting room in the same gentle but firm way a person might ask their spouse to come to bed with them. "There are lots of people there you need to meet."

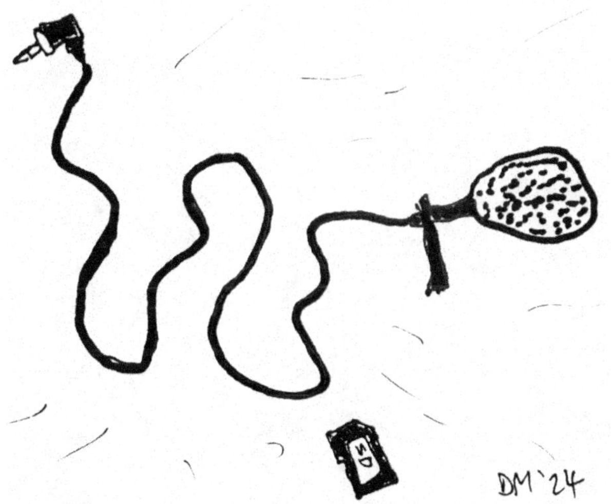
SD
DM '24

You're Melting

Clive looked up at the bench, smiled, and walked towards it. Even from behind, he instantly knew the shape of the person sitting there. Being the groundskeeper at Kingsworth's largest cemetery, you got to know the regulars, and no one had been more regular these last three years than Ava-Mae.

"Morning!" Clive shouted, not because of the time of day—it was mid-afternoon—but because it was a little joke he had with this woman, a slight pun on the fact her initials were *AM*.

Usually, this greeting guaranteed an instant cackle in response from Ava-Mae, but not today. She was silent. The only sound Clive could hear was the slow scrape of a few dead leaves being dragged across the tarmacked path by the gentle spring breeze.

Clive wasn't overly surprised; Ava-Mae's hearing had definitely been getting worse these last few weeks. Much as she did a brilliant job of hiding it behind her incredible wardrobe of bright colours and her sharp tongue, she was old after all. Most of the regulars here were.

The blazing sunshine forced Clive to squint slightly and make a mental note to find his sunscreen—despite working outside all year round, he was forever a pale and pasty man. Even on a cloudy day, he would still turn the pale pink of cooked salmon in no time at all.

Knowing her as well as he did by now, Clive didn't just have a time-of-the-day-based play on words to get Ava-Mae's attention. Like most friendships, running through its core was a pillar of jokes and banter.

Clive switched on the leaf blower and swung it in a wide arc, deliberately blowing air across the backs of Ava-Mae's heels—a trick she pretended to hate but secretly loved.

Still nothing.

He swung the blower back, aiming a little

higher this time, causing the back of her flamingo pink jacket and her magnificent dome of kinked, blown-out corkscrew coils—black sprinkled with pepper—to shimmer slightly.

Again, no response.

That *did* make Clive feel a little put out, but he knew sometimes Ava-Mae would just zone out, deep in memories. *And wasn't it this time of year her husband passed?* he thought. *The anniversary must be close; it might even be today, in fact. She's probably lost in thought.*

He was almost close enough to reach out and shake Ava-Mae's shoulder now, and nearly did. That night, when he woke bolt upright in bed screaming as he relived what he was about to see, he was glad he hadn't touched her.

What kept his hand back was spotting the ice cream just to the left of Ava-Mae's shoe— a couple of drops that had escaped from the cone she loved to bring with her while she visited her husband's final resting place. She'd told Clive a few months ago about how they used to get ice cream together, and how Phillip would always point out when hers was dripping with the words *You're melting*. It became one of those little bits of vocabulary that a marriage—a good marriage—always seemed to generate for itself and use liberally. Clive had since made a point of saying it to Ava-Mae whenever she was sitting with a cone, woolgathering in front of Phillip's grave because it had so much meaning to her, and it always made her smile. He'd gotten a rise from her for it just a couple of hours earlier, as it happened.

Saying it again would definitely *bring her back to the here and now,* Clive thought, *no doubt about it.*

He rounded the bench and as he went, cleared his throat to speak.

"You're melt—" but the word got caught in the horror that had taken over his body and stolen his voice.

Ava-Mae was dead.

By the looks of it, she had not gone peacefully. Her face wore an unmistakable expression.

Fear.

Ava-Mae had perished in absolute and total fear.

Clive gagged, stumbled backwards while trying to turn away and only succeeded in tripping over his own long legs. He felt another urge to retch, but managed to hold it down before scrabbling to his feet and running back to the golf buggy he used to get around the cemetery so he could fumble for his phone and call this awful scene in.

He left Ava-Mae sitting under a stunning spring sky, her dead eye staring into nothing.

Earlier

For such a sad day, it sure was beautiful.

That's what Ava-Mae Morris thought as she meandered slowly from the cafe—ice cream cone in one hand, small purse in the other—and through the cemetery gates. It was a perfect spring day: a clear and confident cobalt sky, bright sunshine that was deliciously warm without having the unbearable heat that summer would bring, and a freshness that evoked positivity—blossom on the trees, a baby rabbit darting off to the bushes, and just the general feeling of the world starting up again.

Of course, it wouldn't be starting up again everywhere. She was visiting a physical reminder of death, after all. That's why today, beautiful as it may be, was a sad day for Ava-Mae. It was the anniversary.

Three years. Three years without Phillip.

Being a widow was not something Ava-Mae readily identified as, but there would be few other reasons for visiting a cemetery so often that you'd made friends with the groundskeeper.

Not that it bothered her. It was actually a nice place to spend time, a peaceful place—away from Kingsworth town centre which, even though it was a sleepy little town, was somewhere she found overwhelming as she got older. Much as she hated it at first, Ava-Mae had grown to love North Hope Cemetery; it was just a shame some kids had run off with the RTH from the sign above the gates.

Ava-Mae continued on her route towards plot nineteen, where she would find her husband. As always, she looked sensational. Save for a sprinkling of pale grey, her afro was still as black and as incredible as it was four decades earlier, framing her face in a way that simply pulled you towards her sharp eyes. Heck, even the flicks of grey added something —they spoke of wisdom, of experience. Of *life*.

She could also always be relied on to bring some colour to No Hope, as the other regulars lovingly called it. Today, she'd *had* to pick the bright pink jacket—it was the anniversary after all—as well as her white trousers and what she saw as her immaculate black-and-gold shoes.

The only things that gave her age away were her gnarled and spotted hands—always the traitors to a human body—the slow pace at which she made her way down the path, and the grimace that involuntarily spread across her face when she sat on the bench opposite the gravestone.

Phillip Randall Morris
21 September 1932–25 March 2021
Much loved, much missed

Ava-Mae sighed, then took a lick of her ice cream and stared forwards, remembering. He'd bought her ice cream on their very first date, had spotted the imminent danger of her raspberry ripple dripping onto her hand and had reached forward and gently dabbed it with a napkin. It was the first time he said those words to her.

"You're melting," Clive, the cemetery groundskeeper said from away to her left, jolting Ava-Mae from her reverie. He smiled at her.

Ava-Mae caught the bit of run-off just before it escaped the cone, then smiled back.

"I keep telling you, Morning," Clive said, using that silly name he'd come up with for her based on her initials, "you've got to be quick when the sun's out. Ice cream first, memories later!"

"That makes it sound like I can separate the two," Ava-Mae said, "but thank you, Clive. Now keep that leaf blower away from my ankles—they still feel the chill even on a day like today."

"Whatever, Morning. You know you love it really!" Clive laughed.

He saluted her, then went on his way. Ava-Mae watched him for a while, then turned back to the gravestone.

And frowned. It had changed. Something had been added.

But that's impossible, she thought. *I must be hallucinating.*

She squinted to get a better look, when she suddenly felt movement to the side of her, as if someone had sat down on the same bench to her right.

"You're melting. Catch it, quick!" the voice of her dead husband said softly in the spring air.

Ava-Mae turned and took him in. There he was —Phillip, looking just as he had a week before he died, wearing his best Sunday charcoal grey suit, a crisp white shirt, and deep red tie. The sunlight caught his dark umber head—a head that hadn't seen a hair trouble its surface since the seventies—and it looked totally magnificent in spite of him being dead; on this glorious afternoon, it looked rich and healthy. His russet brown eyes were staring forward at his own gravestone and so he was in profile to his wife, not giving her the full picture, but she enjoyed the view all the same.

"I thought you'd come today. Your anniversary. That's why I wore this." She tugged at the jacket with her right hand.

"It always was my favourite. Nice shoes, by the way," Phillip replied without turning his head.

"Nice? Phillip, these shoes are not just nice, they are wonderful, they are spectacular, they are ... *immaculate*. And you haven't even looked at them!"

Phillip chuckled, but didn't shift his gaze from his headstone. Ava-Mae looked at him a little longer, then took another lick of ice cream.

"What flavour did you get?" Phillip asked.

"Do you even need me to tell you?" Ava-Mae replied with a smile.

"Raspberry ripple. You never change!"

"I do!" Ava-Mae insisted. "Just not when I'm with you! Raspberry ripple is solely kept for spending time with you—it always has been."

She cackled her signature laugh.

Phillip, still looking straight ahead, said, "I miss you. I miss you so much."

Ava-Mae turned back to her husband.

"I miss you too, darling, like you can't imagine." She paused. "Are you done looking at your gravestone yet? Only I'd love to remind myself of the full glory of your beautiful face."

"I can't," he said.

Ava-Mae chuckled. "Don't be such a tease, Phillip. You don't get to keep teasing me after you're dead. Look at me, honey."

"No. I told you, I can't."

Ava-Mae sighed and joined her dead husband in staring at the gravestone. What she saw made her eyes widen and her mouth drop open in horror.

It had changed again, just like before. And this time it was no hallucination. She couldn't believe her eyes. More ice cream melted over the cone and this time, it did cover her hand, and even dripped onto the ground next to her immaculate shoes.

She looked up and saw the previously brilliant

blue sky was now the colour of carmine, burning with danger and laced with gunmetal clouds.

"They eat me, Ava-Mae," Phillip said from her right. "They won't stop eating me."

Ava-Mae turned and saw her husband was finally facing her.

The right side of his face was raw. It had been chewed at. Where his eye should have been was just a deep, bloody hole. The eye wasn't the only thing missing; a chunk of his earlobe was also unaccounted for, and there were deep scratches all along his cheek. As a tear leaked from his remaining eye, the capillaries in Ava-Mae's own eyes began to burst, turning the whites to scarlet, although she didn't know it.

Her ears filled with crippling white noise—like radio static with the volume cranked to eleven—and she started to lose feeling down the left side of her body.

"They w-w-won't stop," Phillip gargled, before a rat pushed its way out of his mouth and flopped onto his lap.

Then something began to ripple under his shirt. Ava-Mae heard her own pulse pounding like a drum in her ears, thumping against the still-raging crackle of white noise, to the point where it started to hurt, before Phillip's shirt burst open and a stream of rats poured out of his torso and rushed towards her. Some had even gnawed their way through the back of his jacket and had climbed over his shoulders to join the rest of the horde.

She flinched backwards—somehow still holding her ice cream—then vomited over her chin. At the same time, her nose and ears started to bleed. She scrunched her eyes shut.

The white noise stopped, turned off like a tap, but her pounding pulse kept the beat.

"Don't look them in the eye."

This time, Phillip's voice came from her left, between the bench where she was sitting and his grave. She snapped her eyes open and the rats were gone. She turned and faced Phillip, but saw something terrible in her peripheral vision.

Hooded figures, dozens of them on either side of her, edging closer. With every step they took, she felt the pressure in her temples increasing, and the sky changed from red to purple.

It was unbearable.

"Don't look at them, darling," Phillip said, now sobbing from his good eye, his own gravestone visible through the cavity in his body created by the rats that she was no longer even sure had been there, while his jacket and tie flapped in a wind that had definitely not been blowing five minutes ago.

North Hope Cemetery was no longer a peaceful place. It had shown its true face as a place of death.

"Don't look at them," his mangled face repeated.

Again from her peripheral vision, she saw the figures pushing their hoods back one at a time, giving the light an increasingly orange hue. Each hood being removed added more pressure to Ava-Mae's temples before it moved behind her eyes.

Even without looking at them properly, Ava-Mae knew that what was under those hoods was terrible. She knew that to look at any one of them would drive her insane, yet her body was trying to turn her eyes that way. Ava-Mae kept resisting, and the pressure across her face grew and grew. When the final figure disrobed, Ava-Mae's left eye ruptured with a sickening *pop* and the remains ran down her face, trickling slowly like jelly on ice cream.

Phillip appeared directly in front of her face,

close enough for her to smell the three years he'd spent underground. It was foul.

The first scent to hit her nostrils was of spoiled meat, laced with something sweet, like gone over peaches. But the smells beneath it were worse. They were a putrid, nauseating blend of garlic, rotten cabbage, excrement, and a familiar, musty note that Ava-Mae placed after a beat; mothballs. Her brain processed all of this in less than a second, and her remaining eye stayed on Phillip the whole time.

He was crying and laughing hysterically at the same time. He caught the gaze from his widow's remaining eye and spoke clearly.

"You're melting."

Ava-Mae finally dropped her ice cream. It landed on her immaculate left shoe and splattered across to the right. At the moment of impact, everything vanished—her deceased husband and the hooded figures, the grotesque sky, dark clouds, and strange light—and her heart exploded. She expired without even feeling it.

There was vomit on her bottom lip and chin and paths of blood running from her nostrils to her mouth as well as out of her ears. The dribbled remains of her ruptured eye continued to ooze slowly down her cheek; her left hand was covered in melted ice cream. Her blood mixed with the raspberry ripple sauce that ran through the vanilla, which popped against the warm sepia skin of her hand. There was more ice cream on her pristine black-and-gold shoes.

Straight ahead, her dead eyes stared at her husband's gravestone.

Phillip Randall Morris
21 September 1932–25 March 2021
Much loved, much missed

Ava-Mae Morris
17 May 1934–25 March 2024
Together at last

North Hope seemed to take a moment to catch its breath. A single drop of blood fell from Ava-Mae's nose and landed right in the middle of her spilled ice cream on the tarmac under her feet. A bird flying overhead squawked loudly. A tractor cruised past the entrance to the cemetery, its large wheels sending a deep note that seemed to shake the very earth. In the distance, the sound of the groundskeeper's work boots clomping on the foot-path indicated he was heading back towards plot nineteen.

A rat poked its head from behind the grave-stone, sniffed the air, then looked at the slumped body of Ava-Mae. It smelled everything: the blood, the vomit, the ice cream. It felt brave enough—hungry enough—to start moving towards it.

"Morning!" Clive shouted from behind the bench and the rat scarpered, burrowing into the earth in front of the Morris headstone and digging furiously to the sweet sanctuary below.

Time Capsule

The bright, friendly banner that hung across the entrance to the Town Hall rippled slightly in the early spring breeze.

1624–2024: 400 AMAZING YEARS!

Its chunky black letters proudly popped out from a yellow background as it flapped against the front of the building.

Gathered under that banner was a disappointingly small crowd. Well, the folks at the Council were disappointed at least—but most people living here couldn't give a shit about their town turning 400, not even with a best-selling author standing on stage to help mark the grand occasion. That, and with the ongoing uneasy transition back to 'normality' and the continued unknown horrors happening on the other side of Europe and in the Middle East, people just seemed to like being at home right now.

Oh, and there was the weather, of course.

It was shit.

That was the problem with forming a town on April 1st, other than it having the stupid name Foolsden: the weather ... April weather. One year you might get blazing sunshine, another your traditional April showers, occasionally even snow.

Today the sky was the colour of gunmetal, the air was cold—February levels of cold—and there was a fine drizzle adding an extra layer of misery to it all.

Those who *were* in attendance were happy enough with free fizz and chocolate brownies courtesy of the council. And also a chance to get a close-up look at Evan Sage Mulligan, the quiet girl from the road that bordered the park who left town to make it as a writer, and incredibly, did just that. She'd not just made it beyond Kingsworth— the 'big' town up the road that was only big until you saw somewhere else, then you realised it was tiny—she'd actually made it out. All the way out.

Like most famous authors, Evan Sage was unremarkable to look at; living in London and travelling the world these last few years had certainly helped when it came to her personal styling, but beneath the designer coat, shoes, and haircut was just another Foolsden face—downtrodden, uninspired, and just a bit, well, flat. Not fed up with life, but not invigorated by it either.

Evan Sage's most striking features were her eyes, which stood out even from behind her designer specs, and her pout, which was unintentional and unavoidable. The old folks here—who made up the majority of the gathered crowd—would all *swear* she hadn't changed since she was a kid. Evan Sage would dispute that with vigour, as you would expect from someone who had done their best to leave their hometown in the rearview mirror for as long as she had.

As it happens, if you held up a photo of Evan Sage from her teenage years next to her face now, you could make a case for her both having changed and not. The styling was fancy, but there was no mistaking the glare and those pursed lips.

Five bestselling novels and three award-winning movie adaptations of them since last leaving

Foolsden, Evan Sage Mulligan was one of the biggest names in horror—ironically, a title she shared with a Kingsworth native, Seren Blackwood, whose story is one for another time— and a welcome boost for the minuscule tourism offerings of her hometown. By welcome boost, that actually meant she *was* the tourism offering. A mini-industry of sightseeing tours, books penned by local historians, imitation blue plaques, and plenty more besides had spawned around town; likewise the "experts" willing to offer the inspiration behind the terrors of Evan Sage's work.

The irony of why she actually wrote horror was not lost on Evan Sage. It wasn't the creepy woods on the edge of town that eventually wove their way into Kingsworth, or the series of unsolved killings that happened during the First World War, or even the supposedly haunted school house.

It was simply boredom.

Boredom of living in a bland town, where people were happy with their lot and unwilling to dare to dream. Boredom, exhaustion, and exasperation of being, as far as she could tell in her teen years, the only local girl who was Black and gay.

I guess I should be grateful something got me

out of here, she thought, *I could have ended up like them, still here, still miserable, pining for what might have been while I counted down to either my next payslip or death—whichever came first*, then snapped back to the present when someone from the council delegation behind her coughed.

Like it or not, she was back where it all began, standing next to the mayor, getting cold and wet and ready to do what everyone was here for—open that bloody time capsule.

The mayor—his cheeks more than a little red in the chilly afternoon air thanks to the drop of bubbly booze on an empty stomach—tapped the mic and grinned too widely. Evan Sage thought he might even have swayed just a little. *Maybe he started early*, she thought, then bit the inside of her cheeks to stop that sarcastic inner voice translating into a smirk for all to see.

"Well, everyone, it's time at last," the mayor said, "As we celebrate Foolsden's four hundredth birthday, we can finally open the time capsule that was buried here all those years ago to mark the creation of a new place to live—and I'm so happy our most famous daughter is here to help us!"

He turned and winked at Evan Sage, who

maintained her polite poker face with great diffi-culty. She did not like the man at all: his greasy hair that was very obviously dyed, the dry skin on his forehead, his slightly-too-long fingernails that pinched you when he shook hands, not to mention the toxic blend of bad aftershave and body odour that you were treated to when he leaned in for a celebrity-style peck on each cheek.

Evan Sage was already looking forward to kill-ing him—ending him with something sharp in his wrinkled pink neck, that she'd gleefully yank back to let him bleed out. She'd simply stand there and watch him fade—relish the scene as his pompous, chubby form would shrivel to a quivering wreck on the floor as his blood splashed all over her shoes. She might even lick the weapon for effect, really go for it.

All via her words on the page, of course.

And I wouldn't let that prick's blood get on my shoes, she told herself, *not* these *shoes anyway.*

There was a smattering of applause and Evan Sage pulled herself back to the present. She smiled awkwardly and nodded. *Most famous daughter* was cringeworthy, but she'd been introduced with worse. Far worse.

Nobody had paid much attention to the time capsule for the last 397 years. Not until the primary school kids did a project on it, which was covered by the local rag—the terrible *Weekly Fool*—and suddenly a buzz started. A buzz for the media landscape of Foolsden, anyway, which meant a paper with something other than stories about potholes, cake sales, and the never-ending campaigns to improve the local bus service and re-open the train station.

The story had found its way to Evan Sage's Instagram feed one lonely evening when she was scrolling aimlessly and sipping red wine. It was a bad and dangerous combination. She shared it to her Story with something profound like, 'Here's something cool from my home!'—a post she had soon regretted.

The Council's instant charm offensive had gone to Evan Sage's agent initially, and looked as though it would, smothered and pushed away in a flurry of polite emails full of words like 'schedule', 'commitments', 'would love to', but that actually meant 'please fuck off.' Then, they realised they could bypass all that by just asking Janet in the events team to chat to the author's mum about it at their next Women's Institute meeting.

Once Evan Sage's mum was involved, the return of Foolsden's most famous daughter was a done deal.

Naturally, Evan Sage's mum was here—although quite where, Evan Sage had no idea. Her agent, on the other hand, was nowhere to be seen. The thought of joining his client and attending this cute little event sounded great in theory, but when it became clear that it would involve *leaving* London for more than two hours, something *Really Important* came up and he had to decline the invitation—with regret, of course. *Schedule, commitments. You know it is Ev?*

So, no agent in the front row for Evan Sage to focus on, but plenty of familiar faces had turned up. Faces from her past, faces she'd seen every day in her childhood, faces that were long over her fame.

Faces that only care now that I'm famous, her brain quipped, *and even then, I'll bet most of them are only here for the free booze.*

Behind the front row, she didn't recognise as many of the gathered horde. Those clutching copies of her books marked themselves as outsiders, but she didn't mind—a few autographs and selfies were a small price to keep her fans happy. Towards the back of the crowd, those gathered just seemed to merge into one, apart from one figure off to Evan Sage's left, whose coat grabbed her eye. It was incredibly similar—nigh-on identical—to Evan Sage's favourite from her teen years: mustard yellow with a huge, thick hood lined with black faux fur, and large pockets on the front.

Trapped with nostalgia, Evan Sage lingered on this figure, willing them to turn around and face her. Why her blood had run cold at the sight of that coat, she couldn't say, but she was desperate to see who was wearing it. Slowly, the figure in yellow began to turn and—

"Of course," the mayor barked, snapping Evan Sage back, "the contents of this time capsule—and the people who left it—are as mysterious as an Evan Sage Mulligan novel!"

Idiot, she thought as the mayor laughed at his own attempt at humour. *I don't even write mysteries.* Anyone watching closely enough might have spotted her fingers twitching at that point, but no-one did.

Idiot, her brain repeated for good measure, feeling very pleased with itself.

The mayor continued to waffle, "there are absolutely no records of what was in the capsule, nothing even to offer any *clues*. All we town officials know is that it was supposed to be opened today. So, let's have our celebrity guest do just that!"

The mayor stepped back from the podium to welcome Evan Sage to the mic. Another ripple of applause passed through the crowd.

"Thank you," she mumbled into the microphone, before her voice found its volume switch and turned itself up. "I'm much better with words when they're on the page than I am when speaking them aloud, so I'll just get on with it."

There was a polite smattering of laughter from the first few rows, but most people just wanted her to finish so they could see what was inside, then go home, get warm, and grumble about a wasted day over a mug of tea. Evan Sage glanced up to look at the person in what she was already thinking of as her old coat again, but they had vanished.

She lifted the time capsule—which had been handed to her earlier and she'd cradled since—for the crowd to see, then placed it on the podium.

"Let's see what was left behind for us!"

The capsule was made of very old kiln-fired clay, and a very new metal hammer—acquired from the local hardware shop that morning, using town funds—didn't take long to deal with it. The heavy tool exploded the old thing, sending shards everywhere. The sound was delicious, and seemed to grab the attention of everyone there. Normally, that unmistakable noise of pottery smashing would be accompanied by a feeling of dread—childhood memories of special things broken by accident and punishment to follow. But this was a permitted demolition, and the loud crack of the hammer hitting the capsule, followed by the tinkling of the shards dropping from the podium to the ground was almost as tuneful as a windchime in a delicate breeze. The crowd was fully engaged in the afternoon's proceedings for the very first time, and turned into a single-minded mob of open-mouthed rubber-neckers. Their eyes widened as one and they all craned forwards to see what this old piece of clay had been hiding under the dirt for four centuries.

That felt good! Evan Sage thought, *maybe my*

next book can have someone who murders people with a hammer.

Evan Sage revelled in the feeling of destroying something for a change, rather than creating it. But, that good feeling disappeared when she looked at what had been inside for all those years.

No, she thought, *no that can't...that's not...surely not...*

But, it was.

Inside, now exposed to the elements was a severed human hand—a woman's hand, given its small size, cared-for nails and delicate, thin fingers—and its clay coffin had kept it remarkably well-preserved. It was a little mouldy, and kind of grey, but otherwise intact.

A few people in the front row caught sight of the hand and went pale. The figure in the huge mustard yellow coat stepped back into view from wherever it had been hiding and manoeuvred its way to within a few metres of the stage, flanked by six others in matching outfits, who had literally appeared out of nowhere. They moved quickly, efficiently, and without bother from the crowd. In fact, it was almost as though the figures had passed right through those folk watching. They'd certainly wove their way to the front without even brushing the sleeve of any other audience member.

Evan Sage didn't notice. She'd seen what the hand was holding. It filled her with dread and set an alarm blaring in her head. Her palms got sweaty, her throat tightened, and her left eye twitched uncontrollably. She felt as though she wanted to throw up, wet herself, and laughed wildly all at once.

Between those dead fingers was a note. Even without being able to read what was written on it, Evan Sage recognised the handwriting instantly.

It was *her* writing.

Without thinking, she plucked the note from the dead hand and read it. As she did, more people in the crowd seemed to take notice, and a looming silence floated over them.

On the note there were seven words and a signature, a signature that looked exactly like Evan Sage's own.

She who returns shall never leave again.

Evan Sage dropped the note and staggered backwards from the podium. She felt woozy and there was a high-pitched ringing in her ears. The bright, friendly banner continued to slap against the Town Hall above her head, only quicker and harder than before. It was matching the thudding heartbeat Evan Sage could hear—and feel—pounding her eardrums. Each time the banner hit the building it was as though an unseen hand—maybe a dead, severed one that had been hiding underground for 400 years—was cracking her across the face.

Slap! Slap! SLAP!

The figures in mustard yellow pushed back their hoods. No one in the crowd saw.

This has to be a prank, she thought. *Some misguided attempt at a joke, surely. Someone trying to create a scene that wouldn't be out of place in one of my own books. They'll all shout 'APRIL FOOL' in a second, then bring out the real capsule.*

Nothing happened for nineteen seconds.

The mayor waddled forwards, not out of concern for his guest of honour, but through sheer nosiness. He hastily plucked the note from Evan Sage's limp grip, read it, frowned, then cleared his throat—a sound amplified by the microphone. That made more than a few people in the crowd jump. He'd gone a strange shade of green.

"Well, this isn't what I was expecting," he said, and chuckled without humour. "Folks, can you just bear with us for a moment?"

Evan Sage looked up with hope for a brief moment, only to find she was being roundly ignored. It appeared no other capsule was coming.

This is *the real thing*, Evan Sage thought while trying not to panic, but starting to panic all the same. Her guts swivelled again, and she chewed her lower lip until they calmed.

The mayor turned to his staff, who were already passing the note around and snatching glances at her. Evan Sage said nothing. She was trying to control her breathing—in for the count of four, out to the count of eight.

It helped. Until she happened to glance up and see not only the figure wearing her old coat, but another three on either side of it. She blinked, and when she opened her eyes, they were gone—but they had been there; her thumping heart told her that much.

"I'm...I'm sorry, but I need to leave," Evan Sage said, but it came out in barely more than a whisper. "I need to get out."

No one heard. Or, if they did, they ignored her.

Evan Sage scrunched her eyes shut, counted to three, then opened them again. This time, there was no doubt: seven figures wearing her favourite old coat, all of them with the hood pushed back to show a familiar Foolsden face—her face. Except each one was bleeding—two from the mouth, one from both ears, and three from the nose.

However, the worst was the figure in the middle. It was wearing Evan Sage's face inside Evan Sage's favourite old coat and where its eyes should have been were two holes pouring with blood—gushing, pulsing in sync with the friendly banner that continued to flap against the building above. Every slap brought with it a new flow of blood, like the relentless beating of that sign was pushing the blood around those atrocious, unnatural beings. Beings that looked just like her.

Evan Sage gasped and all seven figures in mustard yellow instantly pointed at her. When they did, Evan Sage felt hot—unbearably hot—and her knees wobbled.

What the hell is happening here? she thought before passing out, knocking the podium over in the process and sending the severed hand into the crowd. At first, as it climbed through the chilly, drizzly air, the hand seemed to move in slow motion. It completed a single somersault that was so delicate it was almost graceful. Then, it reached its peak and succumbed to gravity, at which point, it was as though someone changed the playback to normal speed again. After that, everything happened very quickly.

The hand plummeted into the crowd and slapped an old woman in the face, then landed in the lap of a toddler sitting in a pushchair, who proceeded to suck one of the dead fingers, to the revulsion of the child's shrieking mother. The nearby *Weekly Fool* photographer, however, was delighted; he pointed his lens and started clicking, snapping the frames that would finally make him go viral.

All the while, the friendly banner continued to whip the front of the Town Hall, even louder than earlier.

Slap! SLAP! **SLAP!**

The volume of those slaps was downright disturbing—unnaturally loud. But no one heard it over the screaming as the figures in yellow coats moved in, the figures that everyone else had finally noticed. They moved in unison, their arms raised straight in front of their bodies, and their eyes blazing neon green.

Mirrored

I woke up screaming just like, deep down, I knew I would.

This last year, it almost always happens when I sleep somewhere that isn't in my own bed; instead of having a restful night, I'm sat up, eyes wide open, at a time that you only normally see in the afternoon.

Why? The visions. The voices. That fucking *music*.

I thought it would be different tonight. I thought I'd covered all of the mirrors in this room— clearly not. Once my heartbeat returned to a more normal speed, I got out of bed, looked around, and soon found the culprit: a skinny thing on the inside of the built-in cupboard. That's how thin the line is; miss even the smallest, most insignificant mirror—something nine out of ten people using this room wouldn't ever find—and I pay for it with terror in the small hours of the night.

If you haven't already written me off as crazy, you might be more than a little intrigued about the mirrors and why I have to cover them to sleep—shit, just to *exist*—and I'll get to that soon enough. First though, I want to explain why I'm even attempting to write this down. I'm conscious it'll look like the ramblings of a madman, but I'm sick and tired of hauling this round with me everywhere. The mirrors, Tim Smith, the funfair, Tim Smith, the horns and the drums, Tim Smith, and the rest of that spring day in 1998.

Tim Smith. Tim Smith. Tim fucking Smith. A name that haunts me still almost a quarter of a century on.

Anyway, I was explaining my thought process, wasn't I?

I remember back at school—not long before everything I'm about to tell you about happened, actually—I had an art teacher who told us about a novel way of dealing with recurring nightmares: paint them. Do that, he told us, and you'll stop having them. Some sort of dark magic where by making them real, by capturing them on a sheet of paper, you can purge them from your mind and let yourself sleep easily again.

I tried it as a kid and what do you know, it *worked*. That horrible bike ride, sharp turn, and endless falling from the cliff edge never bothered me again. I'm hoping the same logic applies here. If I write down what happened that day, perhaps I can purge it too. Or turn the volume down, at the very least.

You see, I know I'm safe at home. Nobody seems to notice there isn't a single mirror in my house—or if they do, they're too kind to say anything. Away from home, I don't have that control, and with this new job—a job I'm damned lucky to have—I'm away a lot.

On the road, I'm much more vulnerable to their calls.

And while it feels insane to write, the mirrors are definitely making up for me muting them *chez moi*. They just won't leave me alone, calling me—*begging* me—to come and take a look. And if I do that, I dread to think what I'll see and what state my mind will be in afterwards.

Or if I'll even survive.

I've spent more than two decades thinking the mirrors did what they did simply to help me out—to help me make a stand. Deep down, though, I know I'm kidding myself. Because what they did for me back in '98, they didn't do out of the kindness of their hearts. What they did left me in their debt, and I think they've decided to call me up on it and make me pay it back with heavy interest. Especially now that Tim's has been settled too.

But I can't pay it—I *won't* pay it, at least not yet. It's far too early.

So, this is my attempt to purge Tim Smith and everything else to do with May 1998 from my psyche. I'm fully aware it might not work, and even if it does, it almost certainly won't be permanent. But it's worth a try.

Besides, I'm currently looking at a clock showing a time beginning with a three, and I'm not going to be sleeping any time soon. In short, I've got nothing better to do. So, here goes nothing ...

***

This condition, this affliction, this ... disease I'm trying to expunge from my system by getting all of it down infected me in late May of 1998, when I was twelve years old, that awkward age where you've almost entirely grown out of childhood but are some way off from being an adult—heck, you're not even a bona fide teenager; you're stuck in the no man's land of what's now labelled a pre-teen.

This story starts on a bank holiday weekend in the middle of middle England at the start of half term—a week off school to let you recharge before the final stint of classes that took you into the summer break.

It was an exciting time to be a twelve-year-old. I was almost done with my first year at senior school, and even better, the football World Cup was just a few weeks away. As happens every four years in this country, the press had gotten carried away and everyone was riding a wave of optimism, genuinely thinking England might win the thing.

Because of the proximity of that tournament, there was one song that soundtracked those spring days in 1998: *Carnaval de Paris* by Dario G—a musician far less exotic than his name suggests.

This tune was the official anthem of the upcoming World Cup; though you might not know it by name, you'd recognise it right away if you were there at the time. What started as a warbled jingle played on a trumpet—like a Mexican *Last Post*—then burst into life with samba drums and a huge chorus that was built for the terraces, an infuriating and incessant chorus of whistles layered underneath just to ensure this earworm took hold.

Dah duh, dah duh, dah duh dah duh da-de dah.

You couldn't move for that hook in '98, and it's a sound that haunts my nightmares today. If you don't think you know it, look it up—you'll probably be surprised.

Right, back to the story.

As was always the way for the May half term break in the sleepy Warwickshire town of Kingsworth where I grew up, the circus was in town. Well, not actually a circus; more a travelling funfair. You know the kind—a gang of trailers and caravans take over a small corner of public land for a few days, make a load of cash selling you cheap thrills, and then move onto the next hit.

If you hadn't guessed already, the fair is the setting for this story and I'll get to it shortly. But I'd like to introduce you to my friends first, now that we've covered the setting and the soundtrack.

There's that famous line at the end of *Stand By Me* where the narrator talks about how no one has friends like the ones they had when they were twelve. Much as it's a great line, it never clicked with me.

I found making friends as a twelve-year-old tough. I was the only person from my junior school to go to the senior school that I did, which meant I started life there alone. It was pretty daunting—my new school had its own junior version attached to it, meaning around two-thirds of my new class-mates already knew each other, had for years. *They* were the ones likely to trek off into the woods hunting for a dead body and revelling in the comfort of long-established friendship while they did it.

As for me, I was starting from scratch.

I wasn't alone in that respect; there were other lone rangers like me nervously standing on their own on that first day of Big School. Naturally, we gravitated towards each other and hastily made friends through our shared outsider status.

By the following May, I was part of a band of four former soloists and we'd spent the previous eight months forcing ourselves to spend time with each other—friends through circumstance rather than choice—while we all worked out who we really wanted to be.

Like I said, being twelve is awkward.

My posse was decidedly uncool, but we looked out for each other and I suppose that was something. Next to me you would almost always find Simon, Joey, and Megan—almost entirely invisible as individuals, and to be honest, only mildly less transparent as a collective.

Like me, Simon and Joey were only children. Simon was unfortunate-looking: goofy teeth, thick glasses that magnified his eyes just enough for you to notice and be freaked out by it, and tight, wavy hair that looked terrible whatever he tried to do with it. His voice was awful too, poor kid; the pitch of it made you cringe.

Joey fared better in the hair department—as much as you can when you were rocking mid-'90s curtains anyway—and he had a much better wardrobe than any of us. But those clothes, no matter how on trend they were, never looked right on him, often making him look like someone in their mid-forties. Oh, and he had asthma, so the phallic bulge of his inhaler was always visible in his pocket.

Megan had a younger sister and a short haircut

that, at the time, saw her labelled as a tomboy—despite it being just a short haircut. Being an elder sibling seemed to make her the most positive and most confident of our group and as a girl, she gave the rest of us a different perspective on life and forced us to try new things; we'd all kick a ball around for a bit and then go and try out temporary hair colourings on each other, all in the same afternoon. She was the kind of girl your mum hoped would end up being your girlfriend—at least, that's what *my* mum hoped.

Then there was me, still packing a bit of puppy fat with a face covered in freckles that made me look even younger than I was.

At that point in time, my main style icon was still—tragically—my dad, with his wannabe-rock-star long hair. I had desperately tried to emulate this, but where dad's hair grew down, my dark curls seemed to want to stay closer to my head and just get thicker and thicker. I was usually found wearing really bad jeans with a high waist and cringeworthy cuffs—although, to be fair, we *all* wore terrible jeans—paired up top with something from the merchandise store of Aston Villa Football Club, my team. A year or so later, I discovered band t-shirts, baggy jeans, and black nail polish—I was actually sort of cool for a bit—but back in '98, I was a million miles away from that.

I mentioned it being an awkward age, right?

So that was our troop. Alone, we were painfully uncool and easy targets for the popular kids. Together, we were *still* painfully uncool and, in truth, *still* easy targets.

But at least we had each other.

That May day, we'd agreed to treat ourselves to an afternoon at the funfair. I think that sums us up better than anything, the fact we actively chose to go during the day. The fair was at its most tempting—and most fun—after dark, when its colourful lights gave it presence and mystique. That's when most people went.

That was also exactly the reason we didn't go then. We weren't scared of the dark, but more scared of who we might see from school if we went at that time. Going during the day, we figured, gave us the best opportunity of not seeing anyone.

We would, of course, be proved wrong on that point—and how things might have turned out differently otherwise.

I lived just a short walk from the park that

had temporarily given over its large, flat field to be transformed into the closest thing you'll get to a carnival of delights in the UK, so we assembled there, put up with the fussing of our parents and then finally set off.

Even at the age of twelve, we enjoyed speaking to each other's parents as if we were their peers. We'd address them by their first names, comment on current affairs, and laugh at their jokes even if we didn't understand them. We thought that made us seem mature, not realising until years later that we actually just came across as a bit weird.

However, the other side of being twelve meant that as soon as we were alone, our childish enthusiasm for the rides and stalls we were about to encounter came bursting out.

By the time we arrived at Abbey Park that afternoon, we were flying—eyes wide, tongues running at one hundred miles per hour, and hearts beating wildly with excitement.

"I saw the Helter Skelter on the drive here. I've never seen one so high!" Joey exclaimed.

Megan jumped in, "I know, right? And apparently the teacups are way faster than they're allowed to be in proper theme parks."

"And the people running it don't give a shit who you smash into on the bumper cars," Simon chipped in, subtly reminding us that we could swear and get away with it now that we were out of earshot of our parents. For a bunch of twelve-year-olds, that was a big fucking deal.

"Don't forget the smaller stalls. People always ignore them, but those shooting galleries and Hook-a-Duck stands have prizes on them," I said.

"Like you'll win anything," Simon threw back.

And so it continued, probably with some references to someone else's mum chucked in somewhere. You know, twelve-year-old stuff.

If you're expecting me to tell you how the fair itself was this dark, malevolent thing—a place so sinister and spooky that you almost take it for granted that something bad would happen there—then you're going to be disappointed.

Sure, there's always something unnerving about a strange thing in an otherwise familiar place, and there was a small amount of fear in the air between us as we paid our entry fees and walked into its lair: not only the fear of the strangers running the show and having to trust that they would strap you in tight enough to stop you from being flung from a ride to a gruesome death, but also just fear of losing your lunch, and of returning home with your pockets far lighter than when you went. In other words, normal fairground stuff.

The fair *was* set out like a coiled snake, but that's about as spooky it got.

At its core were the bumper cars and Helter Skelter, while the spiral path towards them was littered with small attractions like Hook-a-Duck and shooting galleries, a few food stalls, and a plethora of mechanical rides that involved spinning you around in one way or the other. Music blared out across the site, and you didn't have to wait more than three songs before someone cued up *Carnaval de Paris* again. Those horns, those drums, that melody were inescapable, although after a while, it kind of blurred into the background.

For the first hour we were there, it was everything we'd hoped for; we had a blast, with no one from school there to see us doing so. We methodically worked our way through the fair, taking our time as we headed towards the centrepiece. We got dizzy, narrowly missed winning prizes, and resisted the urge to fill our stomachs with greasy burgers and painfully salty fries.

Basically, if someone made a movie out of this story, this part would be the montage: smiling faces, bright sunshine, and uplifting music—you can probably guess which song.

Of course, if someone *did* make a movie of this story, it would ultimately be a horror film, but we'll come to all that later.

My unchosen but perfectly adequate friends and I were high on life by the time we reached the fair's centre, laughing, joking, and dicking around. So much so that we almost didn't see them. The people we'd strategically timed our visit to avoid bumping into.

Every story like this has a bully or two, doesn't it? In this instance, there were three, although two of them were little more than accessories to flank the really dangerous one.

Those extras—Ravinder and Pete—are barely worth talking about. They were intimidating, but they at least had some degree of a conscience. They could recognise when things were going too far. The same could not be said for the kid standing between them.

Tim Smith was the face of my nightmares back then, which makes it somewhat ironic that he's assumed that role again for me as an adult. He was more than just your common garden class bully; he engaged in a level of cruelty I'd never encountered before and even at twelve, I knew he was dangerous.

He was also everything I was not.

He was trim and good-looking, his straight blonde hair styled with a touch of gel, making him look at least three years older than he was. He had the confidence that his privileged upbringing—both of his parents were successful lawyers, able to buy him whatever he wanted—afforded him. His clothes were completely on point and they looked good on him, unlike how Joey's clothes fit. His voice was lower than any other boy in the year and there were even rumours he was dating someone a few years older and had lost his virginity to her.

More than all that, though, it was his eyes. Those cold, blue eyes that seemed to be both dead like a shark's and alive with the wild menace of a psychopath at the same time. You looked into that gaze and quickly realised the potential for evil—*real* evil—that lived inside him and just how little he appeared to be holding it back.

That terrible moment of spotting them,

juxtaposed with the incessantly positive vibe of—you guessed it—*Carnaval de Paris* was quite the headfuck. Tim and his flankers were about fifty yards to our left, watching the bumper cars, and hadn't seen us. But because we'd come in the middle of the afternoon, it was quiet—there was no crowd for us to blend into. If they looked around at any point, they would see us. And if they saw us, our day at the funfair would shed those first three letters quicker than a ride down the Helter Skelter.

We needed somewhere to hide, somewhere we could go while those bullies got their fill of the fair and moved on. It was Megan who found it for us.

"Here, in here—let's go!" she said, pointing to a trailer to our right that was practically the definition of nondescript. Despite its prime position in the fair, you would never have noticed it unless someone else pointed it out to you. It was so black you would be forgiven for assuming it was either closed or even the shadow of one of the other trailers nearby. The only sign of life around it was a single orange light bulb over an open door, next to which was written 'Hall of Mirrors.'

It was hiding in plain sight. It was perfect. We darted for it, bundling our way inside.

"Now what do we do?" Simon moaned with his terrible, grating voice.

What else was there to do? We tried to enjoy what was on offer.

I'd always gotten a kick out of the Hall of Mirrors as a younger kid—the way you would be tall and thin one minute, then short and fat the next—and they were always more fun with friends, where you could all laugh at your own warped reflections and caricatures together and make sure no one bore more than their fair share.

The first time I was there, when it was me and my friends, that Hall of Mirrors was completely normal. Amusing for a while, but ultimately lacking in any real thrill and certainly nothing you'd tell other people about. I want you to remember that when I tell you what happened later, when I explain what happened on my second visit to that place.

For what little was on offer to entertain us, we spent a crazy amount of time in there—around twenty-five minutes—before agreeing it would be safe to go back out into the open air and tick off the last few rides. On our way out, Simon pulled ahead of us and happened to notice a nook just by the door that would have been immediately to our left on the way in. He squeezed inside and waited, hoping to make one of us jump when we walked past.

He succeeded—so much so that Joey had to suck on his inhaler to calm down—but that's not why I'm telling you about it. When he'd stopped laughing, Simon noticed the weird position of his reflection as he stood in the nook. Because of the angles of all the mirrors in that place, it looked for all the world like he was standing about half-way into the hall itself, though it was just his reflection. It was a fascinating, and incredibly con-vincing, optical illusion. I slowly walked towards his reflection to try and work it out and it's a good job I wasn't in a hurry, as I walked straight into a mirror you couldn't even tell was there. It gave me a slight bump on the head, but otherwise left me unscathed—it had the potential to be a nose-breaker, though.

"How does that even happen?" Joey said, still gasping a little after his shock.

"No idea," I said, "Physics, I guess."

I fumbled my way back to my friends and we cautiously poked our heads out the door and scanned the area. It was clear. Tim and his crew were gone, so we stepped out together.

We made our way over to the bumper cars, ready to finally ride them, only to be faced with a sign telling us they were temporarily closed. Peering round, it looked like some unfortunate sod had gotten carsick, and the people running the ride were dealing with it the same way they did at school, with the weird sawdust that I'm still not entirely sure how it works.

We decided to stick around and make sure we got our drive, so we looked for somewhere to kill time. The Helter Skelter was the obvious option, but because of exactly that reason the queue was hideously long. However, there was a Hook-a-Duck stall nearby with no one playing, so we headed towards it.

Between us that afternoon, Joey, Simon, and I had all failed miserably to land a single prize. Of course, despite what I'd said on the walk in, it wasn't about the prizes—I had no actual use or need for a *South Park* poster, a teddy bear or a goldfish in a bag—it was about the act of winning. It felt like someone in our group had to come up trumps at some point, the cherry on top of our perfectly nice little afternoon out.

"My turn this time, isn't it?" Megan said with a sly grin. "Shall I show you boys how it's done?"

Joey scoffed at her. "Whatever Meg, whatever. But you're right, it is your turn—time for you to join our little losers' club."

"Don't be so sure, Joey," she mocked, and ruffled his hair on her way past—drawing his curtains, if you like. By the time Joey had fixed his look and stopped tutting, Megan had done it—she'd hooked a duck from the middle of the stall, where the top tier prizes are kept, and had managed it with ease.

"Nice one Meg! Never knew you were a Hook-a-Duck ninja," Simon said.

"There's plenty of things you don't know about me, Simon," she replied, instantly turning red. "God, that sounded filthy! What I meant was ..." but then she gave up, as Simon and I were laughing too loudly. She soon joined in.

Once we'd composed ourselves, the man running the stall turned to Meg and asked her to pick a prize. Without hesitation, she plumped for a digital watch—the kind with a calculator on it that everyone wanted throughout the nineties. She fixed it to her wrist before thanking the man running the stall and we all turned around to head back to the bumper cars.

Instead, we bumped into Tim, Pete, and Ravinder, who had appeared out of nowhere.

"Hey, wankers," sneered Tim. "Fancy seeing you here."

He was grinning the grin of a lunatic and staring at Megan. True to form, he was dressed in a pristine white Kappa jacket—the height of glamour at the time—and had a can of Coke in his right hand. He brought it to his mouth and drank, never taking his eyes off Megan.

"I watched you win on that thing." He nodded towards the Hook-a-Duck stall. "Impressive stuff. What prize did you go for?"

"None of your business," said Megan, with a kind of bravery I was in awe of.

Tim's wild eyes sparkled. "Hey, come on, I'm just being friendly. What did you pick?"

"Like I said, none of your business," Megan replied, but her hands gave her away as the left one unconsciously moved to cover the new addition to her right wrist. Most people wouldn't have noticed, but a predator like Tim absolutely did.

Quick as a flash, he grabbed Megan's left hand and pulled it away, revealing the watch.

"Oh, good choice," said Tim. His wild eyes relaxed for a moment, almost becoming normal. "You definitely chose the best one—nice work."

He let go of Megan's hand and stepped to one side, as if to let us pass. But nothing felt right at that moment. Whatever his body language was trying to convey, his eyes screamed it was a trap.

"Enjoy the rest of the fair, dickheads. At least now, you'll know exactly what time you have to leave to get back to mummy for tea."

He started laughing, at which point his two lugs joined in.

I didn't move, not wanting to fall for it, but Megan's nerves got the better of her and she took a step forward.

Instantly, Tim grabbed her again and pushed himself against her. While staring her straight in the face, he squeezed Megan's left wrist.

She yelped. "Ow! Tim, that hurts. Stop it!"

"The watch," he said, his eyes glazed over as if

in a sort of trance. "Give me the watch or I will break your fucking wrist right here."

Megan did nothing except start to cry. Tim squeezed again.

"I'm fucking serious, you stupid bitch," he snarled.

"OK!" Megan stammered. "Let go and I'll undo it."

Tim released the vise from Megan's wrist and she fumbled the watch clasp open. She took it off, and with clear regret, handed it over to Tim, who smiled. He paused for a moment to examine his new acquisition, then spoke without looking up.

"Happy birthday, Tim," he said, "this will go nicely with that sweatshirt mum got me yesterday."

He shoved the watch in his pocket and took another swig of Coke. He was still incredibly close to Megan, who hadn't dared to move. His eyes moved up and down Megan's entire body.

"You know, underneath those terrible clothes, I reckon you're pretty fit. If you grow out that boy's haircut this summer, why not come and see me and I'll show you a few things that these twats you hang around with won't ever be able to do for you?"

He was staring at her and panting slightly. Megan refused to look him in the eye.

"I've been wondering how you're progressing," he added. "It's difficult to tell just from looking."

Without warning, he thrust his right hand under Megan's top, trying to feel her chest. She was frozen with fear, while Simon and Joey might as well not have been there at all. Then Megan's eyes locked with mine and I saw her pain, saw just how terrified she was, and how violated she felt.

That was the act that broke whatever was holding me back—I didn't even think, I just stepped forward and pushed his hand off my friend.

Unfortunately, I pushed too hard and caused Tim to stumble, which in turn meant he spilled his drink. That pristine white Kappa jacket now had a soggy, brown sleeve.

Tim looked at this mess, then slowly brought his head up to take me in. His face was furious; I've never seen someone so angry. What was most frightening was that Tim's expression was not that of some monster from the deep or masked psycho creeping from the background. No, it was entirely human. His eyes locked onto mine, his pupils narrowed to pinpricks, and those windows to his soul immediately conveyed how much pain he was going to inflict on me. His eyes told me bones would be broken, the soft parts of me left black-and-blue, teeth would be loosened, and there would be blood. A torrent of blood. He might stop short of *actually* killing me, but he'd come close.

I realised then that I was looking into the eyes of the Devil, and he had marked me.

"You"—he pointed at me—"are fucking dead."

I didn't wait to see what would happen next. I bolted.

Without much thought, I ran into the Hall of Mirrors and immediately darted into that little nook to the left. A few moments later, Tim followed. The second he crossed the threshold, the door slammed shut on its own, although he didn't seem to notice. With that door shut, just about all of the hustle and bustle of the world outside had been dampened to little more than a murmur —only Dario G's faint samba samples trickled through.

If Tim had looked to his left at that point, everything would have been different—about that day, about the rest of my school years, and about the life I have right now. Had he turned and seen me, I wouldn't have stood a chance. I was cowered in what was effectively a broom cupboard and had no means of escape.

But Tim only saw my single reflection up ahead, just as I'd hoped, and was drawn to it.

"You're not coming out of here in one piece, prick!" he shouted, and confidently strode towards what he thought was me.

BAM!

Tim smacked full on into the mirror you couldn't even tell was there—hit it with such force, I felt the hall's floor rattle underneath me.

That's when things started to get weird.

When Tim looked up, my reflection was laughing at him. Not me—I was still hiding—but my *reflection*, which was now nothing to do with me at all. Yes, it was a perfect likeness of me, but I was a spectator; the mirrors were in charge.

My reflection continued to laugh and point at Tim, which unsurprisingly, didn't sit well with him. You can probably imagine, then, how he felt when my reflection gave him the finger before stepping left and out of sight.

A furious Tim let the animal part of his brain

get the better of him again and he lunged in the direction my reflection had moved.

BAM!

Again, Tim hit a barrier, this time with a sickening crunch coming from his nose. I could now see Tim's reflection in front of me thanks to the maze of mirrors in that place, and I have to say the sight of his blood oozing from his mangled nose made me feel pretty good, especially when some dropped onto his Kappa jacket and mixed in with the still-damp brown stain I'd inadvertently put there.

At that moment, the lights in the hall began to flicker on and off. From the depths of that place came the unmistakable opening drum beat of that stupid song. At first, it sounded like it was coming from outside, but then it kept looping and getting louder, cracking through the air in time with the flickering lights.

The drums finally reached a crescendo and the lights settled. I shuffled out of my nook and lingered near the exit, where I had a clear view of Tim, but he couldn't see me.

Tim was busy wiping his nose with his sleeve and hadn't noticed what now surrounded him: his own form, reflected seven times, and all of them with their backs to him.

He finally looked up and saw them, clearly taken aback a little, but otherwise nonplussed.

Until those reflections started to face him.

One by one, each of the Tims in the mirror turned towards him, all with sick grins on their faces. The real Tim stared at them, with an expression that switched from confused to downright horrified in a second, when the reflections all started bleeding from their eyes.

Before there was any time to process what was happening, all seven reflections suddenly jerked upwards from their necks and appeared to be hanging, faces purple and swollen, vomit on their own increasingly stained Kappa jackets.

The real Tim made a whimpering noise—I could tell he was just managing to hold back from crying. Then the hanging Tim reflections vanished, only to be replaced by a quite horrible scene: Tim's parents, who I'd seen at a parents' evening, and his sister, who we knew from a few years above us in school, all of them dead and bloody—butchered into dozens of pieces by some unknown maniac.

Tim finally lost the battle against his tears,

while *Carnaval de Paris* continued to loop in the background, only a little louder now. The reflections vanished again, this time replaced by another image of me—not looking at Tim, but instead trying to slip away unnoticed.

The real Tim saw it and started to follow, carefully this time. However, before he could get close, my reflection was grabbed by a hooded figure. The mirrored me started struggling and looked directly at Tim, eyes wide with horror, as the hooded figure pulled out a knife and slit its throat.

You've probably never witnessed your own murder, have you? I wouldn't recommend it.

The music dropped a touch in volume. Tim tried to back away from the hooded figure, but tripped over his own feet and sat down with a thud. The figure started to move towards Tim, who was frozen with fear, only able to sob quietly. The lights dropped again for a split second. When they came back on, the figure was even closer to Tim, looming down on him.

At that moment, the reflections changed again —this time, a close up of Tim's crotch multiplied by a hundred, so there was no doubt that he was pissing himself. Tim looked at his own reflected embarrassment and moaned with shame, then snapped his head back up to see where the hooded figure was.

It had vanished.

Wasting no more time, Tim stood up and tried to take his leave, edging towards the exit.

BAM!

Yet again, he hit a mirror, this time making his jaws snap together.

As he tried to gather himself, another sound rumbled out of the darkness of the hall. It was Tim's name, chanted over and over again.

Tim! Tim! Tim! Tim!

As the chanting got louder, a hooded figure appeared in every mirror, forming a circle around Tim. In an instant, their eyes glowed red and they moved, one step at a time, towards him, still chanting his name.

The boy in the middle of that circle was crying loudly now, his eyes dancing in all directions as he looked for a way out. There wasn't one. The hooded figures—those awful, floating red eyes— kept moving towards him.

Then the lights went out and the hall was completely silent. Well, not completely. I could hear noises from the rest of the fair outside, but it sounded a long way away—almost like it was coming from another world.

The loudest sound in that darkness was Tim's sobbing and hitched, frantic breathing.

It stayed pitch black for a count of three, before the thrilling finale.

At once, the lights were flashing on and off, that damned song was blaring its catchy, terrible, jingle at full volume, and Tim was surrounded by hundreds of reflections of me—all with red eyes and each uniquely warped and bent in the way you'd expect in a hall of mirrors.

The music was unbearably loud, but not loud enough to drown out Tim's screams, which cut through the room like nothing I have ever heard before or since.

Then it stopped. The music died. The actual mirrors themselves completely disappeared, taking their ghastly reflections with them. All that was left was a large, empty truck with a scared boy huddled and shivering on its floor, a single spotlight above him.

What I did next, I always thought I did on impulse, but now I realise it was a sort of an encore from whatever force was in those mirrors. *They* pushed me to it.

My feet walked me towards Tim, then my knees bent, and I crouched down to this now-ruined pre-teen. I put my hand on his shoulder and he nearly jumped out of his skin.

I rolled him over and saw a look of unadulterated horror in his eyes when he saw it was me. He was trembling with incredible force and he didn't look like Tim usually did. I was no longer looking at the shark, the beast, the feared predator of my school day. Instead, I was looking at a boy. A powerless, pathetic shell of a boy whose designer clothes and trendy haircut did nothing to stop him from looking weak and scared.

I looked him square in the face and said softly, "Never bother me or my friends again."

At that instant, the door to the hall flung open, and Tim scrambled out.

I watched him run away and then happened to look down. Megan's watch was lying on the dusty floor. I bent down and picked it up, tucking it safely in my pocket.

I made my own way to the exit, but turned around to glance back just as I reached the door.

Everything was as it had been—as every other punter at that fair would have seen it—just a plain old hall of mirrors. The only thing that was out of place was the sound. For once, it wasn't that fucking song, although I might actually have preferred it if it had been—not that I knew it at the time.

There was whispering, from the mirrors. Whispering, to me.

You did it. You did it. Well done.

I smiled, turned around, then pushed the door open, my mood only briefly altered when I heard one final whisper before I left that place. I heard three words that chilled me to my core.

We'll see you.

I left the hall of mirrors and stepped outside, just in time to see Tim rushing back towards the fair's exit, his two goons following with a confused look on their faces. I watched them go, then spotted my own goons by the bumper cars.

I headed over and joined them in the queue, handing Megan her watch. I didn't try to offer an explanation, and none of them were confident enough in our fledgling friendship to force it out of me.

I just told them I thought we would be OK from now on.

***

After that, Tim never did bother us again. Truth is, he never bothered *anyone* again. Some of his old character came out in the heat of battle on the rugby pitch, but the rest of the time he was a shadow of his former self—a mirroring, I guess.

The effect of that day showed in his appearance, too. The strutting, confident posture vanished, and it isn't too much to say that he aged. His hairline started receding before he was fifteen, and by the time we were ready to leave the classrooms behind for the last time three years later, he looked like someone deep into middle age.

But the biggest giveaway was his eyes. They no longer had the wild gaze of a madman. They no longer had *anything* wild about them. The fire was out and they were dead. Not dead like the shark he'd previously been, just dead. One look and you knew something terrible was haunting him.

For me, it couldn't have been more different. From that day on, my social standing grew and grew, and I started to succeed in everything I did: exams, with girls, every hobby I tried out—it all fell into place for me for the next ten years or so.

I never explicitly told anyone what happened in that Hall of Mirrors, but they wouldn't have believed it anyway. There's every chance *you* still don't. All that people knew for sure was that Tim and I both went into that building, and they saw how we both looked when we emerged back into daylight. Tim had pissed himself and stumbled out crying and bleeding, while I walked out tall, proud, and with a new glow in my cheeks. I'd stood up to the person no one had ever dared stand up to.

Various rumours quickly spread around school about what I did to Tim in there, and well, I let them—why wouldn't I? As long as I didn't linger near any mirrors for too long, I was fine. Not that they were calling to me then, but after the experience I'd had that day, they just *unnerved* me.

My 1998 friends and I, unsurprisingly, drifted apart as we hit our teens and found our true tribes within our year group.

Joey got into athletics despite his asthma, and as he grew leaner and stronger, those nice clothes sat much better on him—and he'd even ditched the curtains by the time we packed off to university, too.

Simon couldn't really do much about his looks or his voice, although the latter did improve dramatically once it broke. As the noughts went on, he became sucked into the world of computers, message boards, and other kinds of coding geekery; he was one of those kids who could get past the firewall on the school internet in a heartbeat, which earned him respect, if not admiration.

Megan turned into the young woman my mum knew she would: kind, intelligent, reliable and, in the end, incredibly popular. She and I stayed friends the longest and even shared a delicious kiss at a party one night, but lost touch after school.

As for me, I just rode that wave of good fortune as long as I could. After school I even managed a few years where I *didn't* think about that day in 1998. The mirrors were quiet and I got on with life. It was a good life. It was only last year when I read about Tim's suicide that things started to change.

In case you're wondering, he slit his throat with a shard of glass. A shard of glass taken from a broken mirror, of course.

Almost immediately after that happened, my life started to fall apart. I lost a series of jobs, I went through a divorce, I had to sell my guitars to pay the bills, people—friends—stopped returning my calls and removed me from social media.

That's when I knew my debt was due and the nightmares started. In those awful dreams, I would see it all again, only mine and Tim's places were swapped—a mirror image of how it was in 98', but with one difference. In those dreams, Tim really *did* have a knife.

Since then, well, you know the steps I've taken to try and delay that payment. Now, I'm here in the early hours spilling these memories onto a page in the hope that it'll make them go away.

Has it worked? If you could see how much my hands are trembling right now, you'd know the answer to that question.

No.

Putting this down on page has done nothing to help.

If anything, the whispers from behind the mirrors in this place are louder than they've ever been. I can even hear the faint thud of music. If you were here with me, you'd struggle to make out what song it was. Not me, though. I know it's *Carnaval de Paris*—the soundtrack to my nightmares.

As if to confirm this, the music is getting louder, those unmistakable drums are cutting through the air of this hotel room. It's all in my head—I know that—but that doesn't make it any less terrifying.

I told you at the start that I dread the thought of one day just giving in and finally looking at what the mirrors have been saving for me. I fear that time is getting close. Dangerously close.

In fact, I've just noticed I'm writing this next to a mirror. A large one too, judging by the size of the bath towel I've used to cover it; no wonder that fucking song is so loud. When I looked at the shape of the mirror, the whispers suddenly became a furious chorus, demanding I give in. There's even a twinkling of light sneaking out from the edge of the towel—flashing, colourful lights like you'd see at a funfair.

That day in 1998, changed the course of my life and gave me so much. But I realise now, it was only ever a loan. I'm due to pay it back—have been since Tim killed himself—and you know what? I can't delay it any longer.

If you get this far, thank you for reading. I appreciate it.

But now, I'm going to stop writing, take down that towel, and see what's waiting for me. I only hope whatever happens next is quick and that they have something different on the jukebox.

They won't, of course, but I can hope. Hoping is about all I have left.

Litha

Litha (LEE-tha): the name given to the Wiccan Sabbat celebrated at the summer solstice, the longest day and shortest night of the year and, in some traditions, a time for battle between light and dark.

St. John's Wood car park, Thursday, 20 June 2024, just after sunset

Melanie killed the rental car's engine, opened the door, and was immediately set upon by the gathered horde.

"Welcome, welcome," a man in his sixties with white hair, surprisingly fashionable glasses, and a kind face greeted. "So glad you could join us on this special night—are you Melanie?"

Melanie smiled and nodded, a little taken aback

to have been swarmed by this group of Boomers, all grinning at her, and all standing just a little too close. They were also all wearing a wooden disc about the size of a coaster with the outline of a hexagon carved into it attached to a rawhide necklace around their throats.

"Yes, that's me," she confirmed, eventually finding her tongue, "and my friends are all here, too."

Melanie gestured towards the other four people who'd, by now, slipped out of the passenger side of their vehicle.

"So, we have Seb, Leroy, Ayana, and Willow," she said, each of her friends either nodding or waving when their name was uttered.

"Excellent. Excellent to have new blood to celebrate with us!"

The kind-faced man laughed. The others wearing hexagons did the same. All except one, who had tried to flip open his leather phone case and only succeeded in spraying a plethora of credit cards across the car park's tarmac, which he was now frantically trying to collect.

"I'm Brian, by the way," he added. "I'm the one you've been emailing."

"Ah, OK. Thank you so much for having us," Melanie replied, easing up a little.

"No problem at all. Come over to our gazebo. We've got tea, coffee, and snacks before we get started."

The silver-haired posse—all still grinning—followed Brian, moving away from Melanie. In the dim light, they looked like a very low-flying cloud floating across the car park. Melanie pushed the button on the key fob to lock the car, then raised her eyebrows at her friends, mentally nudging them to follow.

As well as being friends since university, Melanie, Seb, Leroy, Ayana, and Willow were also business partners of sorts—the team behind the terribly-named *Cultcha Vultchas* blog. Every week, they sought out a new cultural adventure to experience, then wrote it up for their website and watched the ad money come flooding in.

Tonight's activity was one they'd wanted to cover for a while: a proper midsummer celebration of the solstice. But they wanted something more rooted in tradition than the gathering of unwashed, floral garland-wearing hippies at Stonehenge, and a bit of research had thrown up the name Litha and ultimately led them here—a Warwickshire car park just a short drive outside the minor tourist magnet town of Kingsworth and next to some woodland surrounded by a bunch of slightly intense folk, all old enough to be their parents and all with a red glow in their cheeks that seemed to accompany the smugness of early retirement.

A bit of a weird one, sure, but it should still be fun, Melanie thought. *And anyway, we're here now—there's no chance of escape. And why did my brain jump to the word escape? Sure, this all feels a bit odd, but that's because we're newbies in someone else's world. Why might I need to escape?*

The youngsters arrived at the gazebo together and soon had their hands filled with cereal bars and mugs of hot drinks. With each bite and sip, they relaxed a little more.

"My young friends," Brian said once everyone's cup was drained, "I'll go into more details about what lies ahead for us tonight in a moment, but right now it's time for the closest thing we get to a prayer."

While Brian had been speaking, the rest of the pendant-wearing tribe had silently and smoothly formed a circle around their guests. It was a well-rehearsed, automatic move, and it caught the newbies off-guard. The Boomers now stood, holding hands and staring at them—still grinning and still a little too close.

Brian said, "Don't be scared. This is how we greet new friends."

Then the group started chanting a few words set over a bouncing, lilting rhythm.

We are Litha, we are one, hail the great and powerful sun.

The moment the chanting stopped, Brian spoke in a strong voice. "Great and powerful sun, Litha honours you this night and looks forward to welcoming you back into our skies in the morning. As we welcome new life to our celebration this year, we thank you for your gifts."

The group dropped each other's hands and each took two steps back. There was a brief moment of silence, where the group looked younger and almost hypnotised, while the air came alive with excitement, electricity, and a touch of danger— just for a moment, before normality swept across them and they were just a bunch of Boomers wearing homemade jewellery again.

Brian smiled, his white hair still popping out of the darkness. "Thank you all—and welcome!"

He cleared his throat, then continued.

"The summer solstice is a hugely important time for all of us, which is why we named our group after it. Every year, we mark this momentous event in the same way and we couldn't be happier that you wanted to join us—your blog really is wonderful by the way. We're thrilled to be featured on it!"

Melanie, Ayana, and Willow simultaneously gasped and broke out in huge smiles, genuinely touched that someone they were visiting had actually taken the time to check out their work. It didn't happen very often.

Seb and Leroy had not been paying attention, and by the time they noticed their friends' collective swoon, Brian was already speaking again. Had they been more focused, they might have noticed how Brian's smile, when he praised their work, was just a bit *too* wide, how the glint in his eye was just a *little* unsettling. As it was, those little glitches simply vanished into growing darkness and were lost forever.

"In a few moments, we'll split into four groups

and each take a different route through St. John's Wood," he continued. "Along the way, we'll show you some different Litha traditions before coming back together as a group at the summit of Alban Hill, which thrusts out of the woodland. We'll reach the top of the hill in time for sunrise, where we will greet the great and powerful sun as it joins us for the longest day. We'll chant and give thanks, then descend together for something I can guarantee will be truly special...a delicious breakfast!"

There were enthusiastic murmurs of agreement from the rest of Litha's members. Their young guests put on their best smiles—nervous, but excited, despite being very much out of their comfort zone.

"The four groups will each focus on a different Litha tradition, so between all of you, you'll get the full experience."

While Brian had been speaking, the rest of his clan had separated into four small groups. It had the air of some long-established ritual, where everyone involved knew their cue perfectly.

"Ayana, you'll be joining Nigel, Sandra, and Karen on a Litha favourite: our scavenger hunt. We need to find enough natural materials to make hexagons for you and your friends, which you can then throw off the top of Alban Hill at sunrise in celebration of the solstice."

Brian paused to remove his glasses and clean the lenses with the hem of his shirt, then continued. "Leroy, you're in for a treat with Arthur, Julie, and Roger. You'll be helping us find our balance between fire and water—a crucial part of this time of year. You'll trek to a part of the woods where we've already left some large wheels. You'll then set these on fire before rolling them into the pond below. It's a tradition we follow to mitigate the heat of the great and powerful sun and marry it with the water to help prevent drought coming to these special woods."

Ayana and Leroy moved to their designated groups and started to introduce themselves.

"Willow, you'll join Pauline, John, and Bill for something more reflective. This time of year is important for taking stock and burying negatives, so you'll get to explore another special part of the woods: our graveyard of negativity. You and the others will all find something to leave there before climbing up the hill."

Willow took her place with the designated group.

"Finally, Melanie and Seb"—Brian smiled—"you'll join Simon, Maggie, and me for a night of conversation. We are the elder members of Litha and would love to talk to you in depth about our traditions. Together, we'll walk to a clearing we call the speaking circle, which is deep in the heart of the woods. There, you'll get to talk to each of us individually and we will answer all of your questions before completing our own climb."

Brian pulled a handkerchief from his back pocket and blew his nose loudly before sneaking a glance at what he'd produced and then stashing the rag away for later.

"Any questions before we head off?" he asked.

"Um, yeah," said Seb, who started sweating the moment Brian looked at him, "just one, and sorry if it's a silly one...but do you have flashlights or something? It's pretty dark and I don't think the light on my phone will do much good in those woods."

He laughed nervously, and Brian beamed.

"Not a silly question at all, Seb! In fact, it was

silly of *me* not to mention it already. Arthur, can you do the honours?"

Arthur—a tall, skinny man with a strange birthmark on his long thin nose and a bald head ringed with the last remnants of grey hair—nodded, then ducked into the corner of the gazebo. He then popped back up and started handing out large, thick sticks, each with cloth wrapped around the end. He gave one to every Litha member.

"Torches!" Brian exclaimed, "fire is an important part of tonight. We use it to light our way and, as you'll see, for other things during the night's proceedings. These torches will serve us until sunrise."

Seb nodded, then immediately shifted his gaze to the ground, feeling nervous for no tangible reason at all other than gut instinct.

"Let's begin—see you at sunrise!" Brian said.

Arthur produced a lighter from his pocket, flicked out the flame, and touched it to the cloth wrapped around the end of each torch. Soon, the fires burned brightly, giving them enough light to see. The four groups went their separate ways and the march of the Litha began for another year.

Ayana goes on a scavenger hunt

Karen smiled the smile of a proud parent.

"That's great, Ayana," she said. "We've got plenty of materials to make the hexagons for you and your friends to use at sunrise— you're a natural scavenger!"

Ayana peered at the older woman from behind the surprisingly high bundle of twigs, branches, and vines.

"Thanks, Karen! It took me back to when I was a kid and doing treasure hunts in the garden with my brothers."

Ayana chuckled, lost in her own memories for a moment.

"Well, let's catch up with Nigel and Sandra so we can sculpt these things. We've got time before sunrise, and they're a really important part of the ceremony."

It wasn't until Karen mentioned their names that Ayana noticed the other two were no longer with them. She wasn't necessarily surprised; for every bit of an extrovert Karen had proved to be, Nigel and Sandra were the exact opposite. Ayana had wondered at first if they had a problem with her skin colour—a lot of people that age seemed to these days—but it soon became clear they were just quiet.

This is their most sacred night of the year, Ayana told herself, *and you're an outsider coming in for a snoop around. They're out of their comfort zone, that's all.*

"Ayana?"

Karen's voice snapped her back into the here and now. She quickened her pace to catch up to the older woman, who was waiting ahead and holding her flaming torch aloft. It showed a fork in the small path they'd been trudging along since entering the woods.

"We're going to take a left here," Karen said. "It leads to a small clearing that is always full of pine cones and other natural jewels that will really top off what we're going to make for you and the others. Nigel and Sandra have already gone on ahead and will be waiting for us."

"Lead the way!" Ayana smiled, genuinely enjoying herself now.

The unlikely duo veered left and walked single file, in silence, for nearly ten minutes. When she wasn't reflecting on how she perhaps shouldn't be so instantly judgmental of Boomers in the future, Ayana was simply enjoying the sensation of experiencing a woodland in the middle of the night. Everything about it was different, and not just because of the dark. The noises, the smells, the entire air felt like it was from another world—one that most humans never even think to try and see or experience.

Ayana was beginning to understand what was attractive about Litha. It was totally fresh compared to any other kind of religion she could think of and was nowhere near as cultish as she'd expected, either. There were no weird uniforms, no garlands of flowers, or ancient books written in made-up languages. There was just a cute geekiness about the whole evening set against a reverence for the environment. Litha's passion for the solstice— along with the spirituality of their group—really shone through. It was intoxicating.

From in front, Karen's breathing was noticeably rhythmic. In fact, she seemed to be muttering some sort of song or hymn as she walked. Ayana tried to focus on it.

Da da DA-da, da da DA, da da da da da-da DA.

Ayana knew it from somewhere, but couldn't place it. She walked on.

Not much later, the light from Karen's torch moved to one side along with the person holding it and showed Ayana the clearing she'd mentioned. Its floor was indeed scattered with a plethora of woodland gems that they'd be able to use for their rustic hexagons.

There was no sign of Nigel and Sandra.

Ayana frowned, and Karen saw.

"Don't worry, Ayana." Karen smiled. "They won't be far away. In fact..."

Karen's voice dropped to a whisper.

"I think they have a, you know, a *thing* going on. They've probably snuck off for a quick snog!"

She started giggling and it was so infectious Ayana couldn't help but copy it.

"Don't tell them I said anything, though!" Karen said, still tittering, "that wouldn't go down too well."

"Your secret is safe with me," Ayana promised with a conspirator's grin.

Karen's quiet laughter petered out, and she rammed the base of the torch into the soft woodland floor so it stood proud and flaming on its own. The force she mustered to drive it into the earth was impressive—intimidating, even.

"Ok, drop everything you've scavenged here and we'll start sorting out which pieces to use for the hexagons. The other two will help us use the vines to weave them together when they come back," she said.

Da da DA-da, da da DA, da da da da da-da DA.

Ayana's ears pricked up at hearing that tune again, this time sounding like it was coming from deeper in the woodland.

What is *that?* she thought, before shaking her head and focusing on what she'd foraged.

Soon, she and Karen were lost in their task, sorting out the bits of wood by size and also gathering a few pine cones for embellishment. Done by firelight, it had a strangely magical and spiritual quality—it was another behaviour that felt like a ritual, a sacrament even, one rooted in nature, the seasons, and the Earth.

Some time later, Ayana heard the sound of footsteps approaching the clearing from behind, coming through the thick woodland.

"Aha! This will be Nigel and Sandra, and about time, too!" Karen beamed.

She stood up, ready to greet her friends but went pale, her eyes wide.

Ayana's pulse tripled as she stood and turned to see what was there.

There were two figures, but they weren't Nigel and Sandra. They were dressed in long, dark cloaks —either black or forest green—and their faces were hidden by flat, featureless pieces of tree bark that had holes for eyes and nothing else. On their heads appeared to be crowns of brambles, nettles, and other sharpened twigs with still-writhing beetles impaled on them.

"What the he—" Ayana started, before Karen's shriek made her look the other way.

Two more cloaked entities had grabbed hold of Karen. One had a grubby, dirt-covered hand over her mouth, while the other stood in place pointing at Ayana.

Her heart pounding frantically, as though it was trying to burst out of her chest, Ayana slowly turned back to the other two creatures from the woods. They'd stepped into the clearing and were now standing way too close to her.

There was a moment where the only sound was the gentle crackle of the torch and panicked, breathy gasps from Ayana and Karen. Then, one of the beings standing in front of Ayana spoke. Its voice was muffled by the awful bit of tree skin it wore for a face, but its words were still clear enough.

"The sun is not lost; it will rise again," it said, and slowly bent to the clearing floor, its hands reaching for the scavenged collection of twigs and branches. The cloaked silhouette next to it did the same.

"The sun lives in me until then," the first figure spoke again, before thrusting upwards without warning and ramming a branch into Ayana's throat.

The pain was instant and immense as it pierced the skin of her neck and then the cartilage behind it. She felt blood trickle out, matching the tears streaming from her eyes.

Ayana briefly heard a shrieking, fear-drenched cry from Karen behind. She turned towards the sound of the older woman, but was instead greeted with another branch—this one held by the second masked monstrosity, which was viciously thrust into her ravaged neck. The first branch that penetrated Ayana's throat had become lodged about halfway, causing her to gurgle helplessly. The second effortlessly slipped through all the way to the other side, piercing the skin like it was a wet piece of tissue paper. Incredibly, this second assault managed to dodge the parts that would have given Ayana the relief of a quick death—although she guessed her chances of making it out were still less than zero. But, one thing the follow-up branch did offer was a fresh jolt of sickening pain right into the middle of Ayana's head.

Ayana sank first to her knees and then fell to her side in spite of desperate desire to stand up and run. Her mind was willing, but her body was powerless to comply. A booted foot rolled her onto her back and it *hurt*, in spite of the heat and excruciating outrage coming from her ravaged throat. The thick tread of the shoe pressed into the soft flesh around her hip and pinched the skin as it moved her over. She stared into the wooden faces of the two cloaked figures. She opened her mouth to scream and immediately it was rammed full of the things she'd delighted in gathering with Karen all night. She felt flakes of bark and shards of tree stab her gums and lodge in between her teeth. She could do nothing about it but make small, whimpering noises in the back of her throat. Before those noises could gather strength and maybe alert a passerby, they were soon choked off by bits of woodland debris falling back there and causing her to gag. More debris and dirt scattered across her tongue and she tasted the land she was about to return to. That was all she could do, except bleed.

She bled furiously. Her chest was already drenched in her own gore, yet with each of the last few beats of her heart more sticky, crimson goo oozed out of her annihilated neck then followed the contours of her shoulders to pool on the earth that was her final resting place.

She shifted her gaze to the edge of the clearing, the trees barely highlighted by the glow from Karen's torch, and waited for death. Before it came, she finally worked out what that tune was. In what she assumed was some sort of delirium of the final moments of her life seeping from her, she swore she heard again—this time, from inside the clearing. Her eyes widened in shock as everything clicked into place.

We are Litha, we are one, hail the great and powerful sun.

Leroy marries fire and water, part one

The wheels hadn't looked like much at all to begin with. Large, sure—about the size of a tractor's rear wheel—but with plain wooden spokes encased in a circle. By the time they'd decorated them with various leaves and vines from the woodland and the flowers from Julie and Roger's car, Leroy had to admit they looked spectacular—even in just the light of the three flaming torches.

Arthur noticed the young man's satisfied look and grinned, causing his already-wrinkled face to look like a crumpled sheet of paper, as everything seemed to scrunch up to make way for his smile.

"We've done a great job," he said. "It's almost a shame to set them on fire, although I think you'll enjoy the spectacle of that, too."

Leroy dusted the last few bits of greenery from his hands and looked at the wheels again. "Remind me what happens next? After we set them on fire, I mean."

Roger lifted his torch and walked a few paces.

He stopped at the tip of a short but sharp hill and pointed into the darkness.

"Down there is St. John's Pond. Water and fire have long been a key part of any solstice celebration, and what we're going to do here brings them together. As Brian said earlier, it helps counter the heat of the great and powerful sun, and by marrying it with the water, we believe we stop any drought affecting these woods for the next year."

Leroy nodded but looked a little puzzled.

Roger chuckled. "Sorry, I get lost in the more spiritual side of it sometimes. What we're actually going to do is set fire to the wheels, then push them down the hill and into the pond, which brings together the heat and wet and consummates that relationship for the year ahead."

Leroy winced.

"Don't worry," Julie chipped in, "we've got protective gloves to wear—you won't get badly burnt."

Leroy's shoulders dropped and he smiled. "You read my mind!"

Julie grinned back. "Here, pop these on. It's time to begin."

The four of them all donned their gloves, then

Roger and Leroy lifted the decorated wheel and stood it on its rim. Arthur and Julie both took a step towards it, stared for a moment, then set the thing alight with their torches.

The fire took hold quickly and Leroy had to squint from the heat and brightness of the flames. He noticed Roger doing the same.

Arthur raised his free hand and spoke in a booming voice he'd not used all evening.

"By fire that is over the Earth," he declared, "and the fire that is under it, we offer you to the water below and ask that the two of you respect each other for another year."

He nodded and Roger started to push. Leroy copied him while Julie and Arthur watched, chanting as the wheel tipped over the edge of the hill and started to move on its own.

We are Litha, we are one, hail the great and powerful sun.

The sight of the flaming circle rolling down the hill, like a giant Catherine Wheel, was spectacular and spiritually uplifting in ways Leroy didn't think he'd ever truly be able to explain—a whirling blaze of hot light cutting through the darkened woods. It was only bettered by what happened when it hit the water, where it flopped onto its side and its flames were instantly doused, sending smoke into the air and filling the woods with a deep, satisfying hiss.

We are Litha, we are one, hail the great and powerful sun.

Leroy didn't realise he'd joined in with the chant until it was over and he saw the way the three older people looked at him.

"Good, Leroy," Julie praised him. "Very good."

Leroy beamed. He couldn't fully articulate why he felt so proud, so accepted, but it was very clearly there. This weird little ritual had stolen his heart and captivated him completely. "I don't suppose I could light the second one, could I?"

Arthur smiled widely. "Rest assured, Leroy, that you're going to have a key role in our second wheel."

Out of nowhere, the edge of Julie struck Leroy on the side of his neck, just under his chin, with a thick, gnarly bit of branch he didn't even know she was holding. He was unconscious almost immediately.

Willow buries the negatives

It had seemed weird at first—really weird, in fact—but Willow soon embraced it. Quicker than she could have ever expected, burying the negatives became addictive and cathartic.

"It's the closest thing we have to confession," Bill said, "but doesn't bring with it any of that general guilt that underpins Catholicism. Or any of that faith's other *problems*."

"Careful now," Pauline quipped and everyone except Willow laughed.

Willow's guides had taken her on a spiralled path that first circled the edge of St. John's Wood, then slowly edged inwards on each lap. It was a long walk, but it was necessary—according to John, at least.

"It gives us time to really think about what we want to bury," Bill continued. "Unlike a traditional confession, we only do this once a year right before the solstice, so there's usually plenty to get out."

For the first lap of the woods, Willow had been told to simply think of anything negative in her life she'd ideally want to be rid of. Once they caught a glimpse of the car park again and started to move a bit further inwards, they stopped, and Pauline took Willow's hand, gently stroking the back of it from her wrist all the way to her green-and-pink nails.

"You're ready now, Willow," she said. "From this point onwards, we will start to bury our negatives."

Pauline paused for a moment.

"It's really very simple. You let the negative fill your mind— it could be something you've done or something you want to purge. Then you stop, bend down, and dig a small piece of earth out with your hand and hold it. All that remains is to stare at this tiny hole while visualising your negative, before you spit in the opening you've made, then replace the earth you borrowed."

The older woman grinned.

"I'm afraid your lovely nails won't look so lovely come sunrise, but your soul will feel like a million dollars."

They set off again. Willow was hesitant at first, instead watching her experienced companions digging and spitting, as well as occasionally glancing back at her in silent encouragement.

Unfortunately, Willow seemed to have stage fright; all of the negatives she'd thought of at the start of the walk had vanished from her mind and with each step, she felt more embarrassed and more self-conscious.

"Do that one first," John said right into her ear, startling her. "Those nerves you're feeling and whatever else it is that's holding you back—bury them now and the rest will come."

Willow looked at his soft, wrinkled face—his moustache perfectly neat but his eyebrows bushy and wild—and was reassured. He looked like a kind, old teacher who was weeks away from banking his pension but still wanted to ensure every one of his charges made it over the line. Willow dug, thought, spat, and instantly felt better.

John had been right; it had flowed out of her after that, and the night sped by as they went deeper and deeper into the woods. The negatives poured out: that messy relationship with Paulo, the angry tweets she'd sent to her local Member of Parliament, the daydreams of poisoning her neighbour's cat to stop it shitting in her garden, not to mention all those dark thoughts of screwing over her friends for a bigger share of their ad revenue. She spat them out and buried them all.

Eventually, the spiralled path led them to a

clearing. Willow looked up and saw her three new friends looking at her and smiling, their teeth glowing in the light of their flaming torches. They looked proud, which made Willow's heart soar. This whole-hearted acceptance of her and her friends into tonight's proceedings was so wholesome and unlike any other trip they'd covered for the blog.

It felt special.

"Well done, Willow," said Pauline. "You've embraced burying your negatives and are now ready for the next step as we prepare for first light and the arrival of the great and powerful sun on this most sacred day of the year."

Willow smiled and nodded. John and Bill moved to stand on either side of her and silently filled the hand that wasn't holding a torch with one of Willow's. Pauline stood behind them.

"Come, kind soul," Pauline cooed, "there is one more thing to bury."

They walked forwards together into the centre of the clearing. Willow looked at the ground and saw what looked like a hole. Not just any hole—it was about the size and proportion of a grave. Bill and John stopped walking, but kept a firm hold of

Willow's hands. Scratched into the fresh earth was a hexagon, and there was another—this one made of twigs—hanging from a tree directly above.

Silence filled the air.

"I...I don't understand," whispered Willow. "What are we burying?"

"We are Litha, we are one, hail the great and powerful sun," Bill chanted softly.

Willow looked around the clearing looking for anything to calm the terrible thoughts now racing through her mind. She wanted to see anything—heck, she'd even take seeing a dead body ready to be dropped into that hole in the ground if it meant she had a way of escaping.

"Guys?!" Willow demanded in a louder but quivering voice, petrified now. "What are we burying here?"

"You, my dear," said Pauline, before she cracked Willow's skull open with a rock the size of an orange.

Willow screwed her eyes shut as she blood poured into them, then stumbled as the two men on either side of her let go of her hands.

"Please, don't—" Willow started, before Pauline struck her again. This time, the impact sent

Willow sprawling, and she fell face first into the grave that lay waiting in the ground for her. The impact of her body hitting the bottom of the hole left her groggy. She did not move when they started to bury her, but she felt the first pieces of earth being thrown back into the hole, covering her back. At first, they sprinkled and trickled onto her spine with a delicate ripple, before slowly getting heavier and thicker, and arriving faster and faster.

Though barely conscious, she was still alive when she heard them chant. She summoned enough energy to roll over and look up at them, her mouth dropping open to scream. The start of a desperate yell poked out, before being snuffed out by clods of earth falling into it. More quickly followed and she felt it over her tongue and her teeth. It tasted damp, thick, and rotten. When it hit the back of her throat, she retched. Most of the vomit she immediately swallowed and began to choke on it, as it had nowhere to go, but some forced its way out of her nostrils, stinging as it went. Willow let out muffled coughs and splutters, her eyes streaming as she did, all set to the same soundtrack from above.

We are Litha, we are one, hail the great and powerful sun.

Then her face was covered and she knew no more.

Leroy marries fire and water, part two

When Leroy eventually stirred, he was groggy, confused, and sore. He could tell he was on his back, but he wasn't on the ground. He could feel spokes of wood digging into his spine, while leaves and foliage brushed his arms and itched his ears. Everywhere, everything, hurt and the fact that he was lying down on...*something* only added to his disorientation. Despite the wave of hurt that rolled across his head when he did, Leroy forced his eyes open.

Once they'd adjusted to the low light and saw what was above him, he quickly came to and his stomach clenched; Leroy had plenty more to worry about.

Staring down at him were three shadows made real—dressed in dark-green cloaks, each holding a flaming torch and hiding their faces behind a crude mask made of tree bark. Leroy could make out eye holes, but little else—not that it mattered. He had a clear idea who this trio was and the bind he found himself in was testament to what those beasts were capable of. It was only when Leroy pondered what they might do next that he really began to panic.

He tried to move, tried to get up, but couldn't. He was bound to the wheel, spread out like the *Vitruvian Man* and fixed in place not with natural materials, but with plastic cable ties. Every inch he moved, they pinched a little tighter, clawing at the thin skin covering his wrists, desperate to break through.

None of the xyloid beings spoke, but two of them moved out of Leroy's field of vision. He then felt a strange sense of weightlessness, his stomach dropping, as the wheel was lifted to a standing position.

Leroy's brain let the rest of him in on what was about to happen. He did the only thing he could. He cried.

The solitary cloaked form still standing opposite Leroy stepped closer to him and spoke from behind its mask.

"By fire that is over the Earth," it declared, "and the fire that is under it, we offer this to you."

Leroy felt a waft of heat from both sides as the wheel was set alight. The thought of waiting for the flames to slowly flicker over his body, engulf his flesh, and burn him alive was unbearable. He locked eyes with one of the masked maniacs, who saw what Leroy wanted, understood what Leroy *needed*, and offered to him swiftly in an act of evil, twisted mercy; the wooded freak used its torch to set fire to Leroy directly, and the other two followed almost immediately. The flames found Leroy to be most delicious.

We are Litha, we are one, hail the great and powerful sun.

Leroy screamed in agony, the air he forced out shredding his vocal cords like cheese being pushed through a grater as the trio of sylvan psychopaths chanted. His body and his face fizzed, popped, and singed as the fire took hold.

Then he felt himself rolling, slowly at first, before the ground dropped away beneath him and the wheel rapidly picked up speed.

The whole journey down the hill—that final ride of Lerory's life—he felt his body scorching and smelled it cooking. Hitting the water and flopping down face-first into the pond was a blessed relief.

As he slowly sank, his body was still. The pond nudged at Leroy's mouth and soon found a way in. His lungs slowly filled with the cool, murky water. He drowned two minutes later, the water just managing to claim him and leaving him forever still. From the top of the hill came a familiar chant.

We are Litha, we are one, hail the great and powerful sun.

Summit of Alban Hill, Friday, 21 June 2024, just before sunrise

As they pushed onwards and upwards towards the summit of Alban Hill—the sky already growing brighter despite it feeling like the middle of the night—Melanie and Seb couldn't help but be amazed at what they'd experienced.

The conversations they'd had in the speaking circle had been sensational. The three elders of Litha had given them a whole new perspective on life, love, and faith, as well as a new appreciation for nature.

Brian was every bit as charming as the way he'd taken charge in the car park the night before had suggested he would be. He was suave, savvy, charismatic—an obvious choice as the group's leader and figurehead. But the other two had been just as good value.

Hearing Maggie talking about her struggles to settle after moving to the UK from Jamaica as a child, before her first experience of anything remotely Pagan in her early teens changed everything for her.

Or Simon's account of his high-flying career in the city that was ended prematurely by an almost inevitable heart attack, before joining Litha for the summer solstice twenty-seven years ago and never looking back.

Those three—unbelievably fit in addition to everything else—had already reached the summit and were rewarding themselves with swigs of water. Melanie glanced up at Seb and smiled when she saw he was blowing just as much as her.

"Almost there," she said between breaths. "I can't believe how good this has been. I'm going to start writing this up as soon as we get back to the hotel—sleep can wait."

"I know what you mean. Some of what we got last night was incredible. If the other three have anything half as good, we're going to have one hell of a piece on our hands. And that hotel seemed weird anyway—something about the window in my room wasn't right, my reflection seemed off. I'm not sure I even want to try sleeping there." Seb puffed.

He trudged on a few more steps.

"This could be something we sell to a national outlet, you know?" he added. "Maybe even go for an award."

"For sure," said Melanie.

That prospect gave them an energy boost, and they finally made it to the summit. Even with the sun still dosing under the horizon, they could already tell the view was spectacular. This sunrise was going to be something else.

"What do you think?" asked Brian with a smile.

"Wonderful," said Melanie. "It's really wonderful. Thank you so much for having us."

"You've not even seen the best bit yet. We've still got the climax of the sunrise," Simon told them.

"I hope the others make it in time. I get the sense the sun will be popping its head up soon," Seb said, looking around for his friends.

"Oh, they'll be here," Maggie assured him. "Don't worry about that."

Melanie and Seb sat down and were soon lost in thought looking at the view, which grew brighter by the minute, constantly revealing new secrets. After a few moments, Brian placed a wreath of flowers and herbs on each of their heads. He was wearing one himself, as were Simon and Maggie. Where they came from, neither Melanie nor Seb had any clue, but they didn't care. They smiled and breathed it all in.

As the first shard of yellow light broke above the horizon, they heard the sound of footsteps behind them. Eager to see what their friends' experiences had been, Melanie and Seb turned around.

They stared in utter disbelief, their eyes wide. What smiles had been on their faces moments before vanished, as did the colour from their cheeks. They couldn't believe their eyes and yet understood exactly what had happened at the same time. That moment of awareness—of knowing the abhorrent, harrowing truth of what had happened in those woods overnight—left Melanie and Seb paralysed, completely unable to react. Their chests were tight, their shoulders trembled and they both felt their hearts thumping in the middle of their chests.

Joining them at the summit of the hill was not the other members of Litha, but a group of awful, arborous beings. Holding flaming torches and dressed in long dark-green cloaks, their faces were covered with flat pieces of tree bark that had holes for eyes and nothing else, and they wore crowns of brambles—not flowers—on their heads. They were blank, dark, terrifying. What they were holding was worse.

The bodies.

Melanie and Seb were both rooted to the ground and silenced by fear. The great and powerful sun edged a little higher in the sky, shining its light on the ghastly scene in front of them. The extra details afforded by the ever-improving light made them even more horrific.

Ayana, Leroy, and Willow. All dead. All with a hexagon carved into their exposed chests.

Ayana's mouth was stuffed with twigs that had been pressed in so far they had pierced through the back of her throat. She'd died with her eyes wide open in terror.

Willow had clearly been hit on the head with something hard and blunt, but she was also covered in dirt, like she'd been pulled from a shallow grave.

But it was Leroy that was the most unbearable to take in. His body and face were charred and burnt, while his clothes—despite being dripping wet—looked as though they had partly melted right into his skin. The sun and the water had gotten married and he was their bastard lovechild.

Melanie sobbed, while Seb turned to one side and vomited. A twig snapped behind them and they spun around to face Brian, Simon, and Maggie.

Brian, Simon, and Maggie...who were all smiling.

"Don't be sad for your friends. Rejoice at their sacrifice for the great and powerful sun, and embrace these final moments before you both join them." He was calm, his voice a gentle dressing for their wounds.

The sun had risen rapidly, casting Brian in silhouette. Even then, Melanie and Seb could see his terrible, terrible grin.

Then the chanting started.

We are Litha, we are one, hail the great and powerful sun.

Not from the three in front, but from the cloaked monsters behind them. Melanie and Seb turned again to see them remove the bramble crowns and faceless masks and reveal their faces.

We are Litha, we are one, hail the great and powerful sun.

Nigel, Sandra, Karen, Arthur, Julie, Roger, John, Pauline, Bill.

They all grinned, then reached under their cloaks and pulled out their hexagon necklaces, which they slung over their heads before replacing their masks and crowns.

"What the fuck?" whispered Seb with a tremble—like he hadn't done since he was a little boy, shaking uncontrollably while trying to tell his mum about the nightmare that had sent him diving into her bed in the small hours. Then Brian spoke again.

"Language please, Seb. This is our sacred moment."

Brian's face was no longer visible. He was now wearing his own mask of tree bark, only this one was intricately carved to show real facial features. Simon and Maggie wore similar face coverings. The masks were magnificent pieces of art; they were beautiful.

They were awful.

We are Litha, we are one, hail the great and powerful sun. We are Litha, we are one, hail the great and powerful sun. We are Litha, we are one, hail the great and powerful sun.

The larger group repeated the chant endlessly. Melanie and Seb moved close to each and held hands. There was nothing else they could do.

"Great and powerful sun," Brian praised in a strong, loud voice that carried over the repeated chanting, "Litha has honoured you this night and now welcomes you back into our skies on this most beautiful and hallowed morning. Thank you for the gifts of new blood you have brought us this night. Now, we return them to you."

Brian gave a sharp nod, which was immediately followed by the unmistakable *flump* of something being set alight.

Melanie and Seb turned to see the bodies of their three best friends in flames. What comfort they took in knowing that all three were already dead and would therefore not feel the heat engulfing their skin and smell it cooking their flesh was small. The horror at seeing it right in front of Melanie and Seb was paralysing. It caused a strange schism in their minds that straddled the line between thinking this was either a dream or a very dark prank, with the very real knowledge and acceptance that this was happening.

We are Litha, we are one, hail the great and powerful sun.

The burning bodies shrivelled and twisted. The Litha horde stepped forwards, past them.

We are Litha, we are one, hail the great and powerful sun.

From the other side, Brian, Simon, and Maggie closed in. Just like in the car park, they were all standing too close and even though their faces were hidden by those masks, Melanie knew they were all grinning.

We are Litha, we are one, hail the great and powerful sun. We are Litha, we are one, hail the great and powerful sun. WE ARE LITHA, WE ARE ONE, HAIL THE GREAT AND POWER-FUL SUN!

The chanting stopped. There was no sound except for the crackling of flames behind them. Litha had formed a circle around Melanie and Seb, twelve masked figures staring at them. Nine of them held burning torches.

None of them moved an inch, none of them

spoke a word and the harsh transition from them advancing en masse while sounding like a choir from hell was deeply unnerving. Melanie's head darted from side-to-side in panic, convinced one of those damned demons was about to make a move and wanting to catch them before they did—if nothing else to give herself just a moment's warning to brace herself for the end. Seb, on the other, just stared at the ground and sobbed.

Finally, there was movement away to Melanie's left and she slowly turned to watch, grabbing Seb's arm and tugging him around to do the same. It was the decorated figure of Brian who had stepped forward from the circle—taking the role of leader once more. He still did not speak, or chant, but instead pulled the hexagon pendant from the folds of his cloak and held it in front of him as though it was a small trophy he wanted to show off to his friend. As he did, the rest of the Litha clan broke their circle and rearranged themselves into a line behind Melanie and Seb.

Brian ran a finger along the flat top edge of his pendant, and then let it follow the contour of the second edge, as if counting—*one, two*. The rest of the group extended their arms and pointed at Melanie and Seb, who both spun around at the sound of ruffling cloaks. Then, the arms of the Litha group dropped and they stared forwards again, at Brian, so Melanie and Seb let their gaze do the same, trembling as they did.

Litha's leader was nodding, his smile wide and obvious despite being hidden behind a mask. He ran his fingers over the next three edges—*three, four, five*—and Melanie and Seb knew that the group would be pointing at the burning remains of their friends. Only they didn't; instead, those holding torches pounding them on the ground in perfect unison for five chilling.

Thud. Thud. Thud. Thud! THUD!

The group stopped, and Melanie looked back at Brian. Seb appeared to have given up and stood there with his eyes clamped shut. Brian had his finger on the remaining edge of his wooden hexagon, but he wasn't tracing the shape of it. This time, his finger was tapping it—slowly, and methodically. It was a simple act to show a chilling fact to his group.

We're one short.

Then, Brian let go of the pendant, allowing it to fall back against his chest, and spread his arms wide in a silent question.

Who will it be?

Melanie saw Brian watch behind her, then nod slowly. Suddenly, a cloaked figure shoved between her and Seb—jolting him back to the here and now. This figure stood next to Brian and slowly removed its mask. It was Arthur, the kind, skinny man with the strange birthmark and the bald head who, another lifetime ago, had handed out torches to everyone. He was still holding his torch now, and his face was plastered with a smile of pure ecstasy. He looked to Brian who nodded again, then raised his free hand to touch the side of his mouth. He shifted his gaze to the line of Litha members he had recently been a part of, then deliberately moved his hand away from his mouth in a gesture. Melanie knew it as basic sign language.

Thank you.

Without a word, Arthur grabbed his torch with both hands and, still beaming from ear to ear, held it against his own chest and kept it there until the flames took him. For three minutes, he stood and burned. He did not scream, he did not flinch, he just burned. Then, he fell to his knees, before slumping over to one side. The flames continued to devour him, and Melanie was unable to look away as she saw them take that birthmark and that bald dome and consume them fully.

Brian raised both arms to the sky and the rest of the Litha clan slammed their torches into the ground with one final thud. Melanie's fingers desperately fumbled for Seb's again because she knew this was it. She knew what was next. Brian lowered his arms and took a deep breath, his chest puffing up and outwards as he prepared his final sermon.

"By fire that is over the Earth, and the fire that is under it," whispered Brian, "the sun is not lost; it will rise again. The sun lives in me until then."

The moment Brian stopped speaking, his clan plunged their torches into Melanie and Seb. The colour of the fire that leapt over their arms, legs, and faces matched that of the summer solstice sun, which watched gleefully from above.

The screaming was awful, the pain incredible. Both were mercifully short.

St. John's Wood car park, Friday, 20 June 2025, just after sunset

As the minibus pulled into the carpark, Brian stole a glance at the rest of his Litha family. They were all wearing the same smile as him. They were buzzing.

We are Litha, we are one, hail the great and powerful sun.

They gave one whispered utterance of their chant, then swarmed towards the vehicle together. Twelve special guests joining them this year—twelve! More than double the tally from a year before, and that had been a landmark year.

"Welcome, welcome!" Brian said to the minibus driver. "We're so glad you could join us—are you Christopher?"

This was going to be another special night.

Anchor

Throughout everything that happened in the old, Victorian labyrinth that is Kingsworth Hospital—all the *weirdness*—he kept hold of the paper clip. It allowed him to stay grounded, it helped him to see it through, it was his reminder of what was real.

It was his anchor.

Waking up and finding himself in a hospital bed was weird enough. He remembered feeling unwell at work, he remembered going to the first aid kit for some painkillers, and after that, he remembered nothing.

At first, he thought the feeling of being knocked for six was simply the stifling July heat—one of those days you only get in Britain a couple of times a year, but when they hit, *boy* do they hit hard. When he was still feeling woozy after ninety minutes inside his air-conditioned office, he knew something was up. Thus, the walk to the first aid kit and the sudden blackout.

When he next opened his eyes, he was strapped to a gurney in a strange place. Strange because it was a hospital and he hadn't been in a hospital the last time he closed his eyes, but it also had the vibe of a *strange* hospital. Even with as little hospital experience as he'd had—almost exclusively taken from TV dramas, plus one visit as a kid to have a blood test—he still sensed this place didn't feel quite right. It was almost ... thin. It didn't feel totally real.

Before that day, he didn't even know Kingsworth had a hospital.

He was given a shallow veil of privacy in the form of a paper curtain around his bed. There were two sounds he picked out. The first—the closest to him—was the gentle bleep of the heart monitor he was hooked up to. The other, coming from just outside his curtain, was someone sobbing.

It was unnerving.

He could tell that the person sobbing was an adult. They were clearly close by—probably in the next bed. The noise was muted, but persistent and so mournful, it was chilling. They were the sobs of someone who had been crying for hours and still had a way to go. There was no pattern to the sobbing either; a random number of them would fall out, interspersed by a couple of hitched, sniffled in-breaths, then back to the sobbing. Some would be subdued—almost silent—and others harsh, throaty, and full of anguish.

He never did determine who was sobbing or if it had even been real, but he knew he'd hear their cries in his dreams for the rest of his life—they would echo. They would haunt him.

He was still dressed for the office. Someone had removed his shoes, but they'd left his grey suit trousers, white shirt, and green string tie on. He realised there was something in his left hand and glanced down—it was a call button.

Wanting to know where he was, why he was here, what was *wrong* with him and—most of all—how he could get away from the haunting cries of his ward-mate, he pushed it.

Nothing happened. No one came. Just the bleep of his own heartbeat and that awful sobbing.

He tried calling for help, but every time he did,

a crackle of piercing white noise—like the sound of an old dial-up modem—spat out of the heart rate monitor, masking his voice and keeping his cries unheard. He tried again and again, but every time the white noise blocked his yells. It was almost as if that crackled, strange, eerie sound was coming from his own mouth.

This can't be real, he thought. *This must be a weird fever dream because this absolutely cannot be fucking real.*

But it certainly *felt* real—particularly that endless sobbing.

He started to panic. He heard his heart pound, banging its bloody drumbeat right in his ears. He felt himself somehow getting hotter on this already unbearable stinker of a summer's day.

He realised he wanted something within his control, something to ground him in reality. Luckily, he had just the thing.

In his right pocket was the paper clip—nothing fancy about it, just a normal paper clip. He kept it in that pocket because he was a terrible fiddler, and its sole purpose was to be something for his fingers to play with during meetings or while waiting in line.

It had served him well for a number of years now and had even helped him focus, particularly on video calls. It seemed having something to keep his idle hands busy was what his brain had needed all along to just get on with its own work. More than that, it seemed to rid him of his lack of confidence and his performance had shot up as a result.

If only he'd known that at school—his life might well have been different.

He reached inside the pocket and closed his fist around the clip, squeezing hard enough for its tiny metal frame to pinch the skin of his palm. It hurt a little, but the hurt was good. Hurting was real. He sighed, gorging on that pain, on having something normal.

Then the weirdness started again.

First, as if a switch had been flicked somewhere, the room was bathed in a rich purple light—like the colour of a Dairy Milk chocolate bar or the Christmas lights from his childhood—the kind of rich, warm lights that make you think of Quality Street wrappers and '80s movies that you simply didn't get with those cold, modern LEDs.

At the same time that the light hit, music started. It was the opening guitar lick to *Sweet*

Child O'Mine, but a few notes were out of tune and played with no sense of timing. It went slow, then sped up, then briefly hit the correct tempo before warping itself again. And it was just the guitar part; no other instruments joined in. It was excruciating, made worse by the unnatural, unsettling light.

He gripped the paper clip tighter.

The purple light changed to a burnt orange, while the twisted classic rock song moved up an octave, making it even more horrendous. The sobbing hadn't stopped either—it was still there, ambient noise to the whole bizarre scene.

He frowned and squeezed the clip again, savouring the shape of it in his hand. He could feel the two loops, the cut ends of the wire, and the thinness of its metal body pressing down into his palm, pinching the rough yet sensitive skin there, scratching and biting and, most importantly, anchoring him.

The purple light briefly reappeared and then changed to the green of a traffic light urging you to get a move on. The *Sweet Child O'Mine* lick dropped down about five octaves and slowed to a dreadful crawl, like the sound of an unimaginable monster from the deep dragging itself through a swamp, its slimy underbelly sloshing over the gunk and silt, its breathing a constant low groan that seemed to get incrementally louder every few seconds..

He shut his eyes, counted to three, and opened them again.

The light was still green, but this time, filling him with terror, there were silhouettes of what his brain could only process as ancient demons standing on the other side of the curtain drawn around his bed. Each of the beasts' heads was shaped like something between a goat and a bull, with a long nose and two large horns jutting outwards and then up from their temples. Their bodies were scrawny skeletons that almost looked human, apart from their arms. Those limbs were short—ending where a person's elbow would be—and instead of hands were capped with large hooves.

Beneath his ribs, the man's heart pounded in sheer panic, but the rest of his body was paralysed with fright. All he could do was moan in dismay. He swallowed, then moaned again. The figures— seven of them—didn't move, but two small red lights glowed from their heads, roughly where their eyes might have been, if they were human. Those eye substitutes glowed brighter and brighter, fourteen tiny red spotlights beaming on his chest, then slowly moving down his body. They screamed, seven grief-stricken screams coming one at a time, all layering over the previous one, but each with a slightly different pitch, resulting in an unbearable cacophony of vocalised pain.

He was terrified. He screamed back in reply, but those skeletal phantoms started mimicking his own cries so all he could hear was his horror amplified sevenfold. It was excruciating. The horned beasts matched his own screams in length, volume, intensity and pitch, which made his terror-filled note reverberate around his own head so frantically it gave him a headache.

He snapped his eyes shut again and clamped down on his paper clip once more, trying not to imagine there being even more of those creatures behind the seven edging towards his bed, lurking farther back in the room or maybe crawling across the ceiling like a spider-demon hybrid that would inevitably defy gravity and probably be able to spin its head a full 360 degrees.

The paper clip pinched and bit and scratched

even harder. It was the only thing that gave him the confidence to force his eyelids open again and see what was before him.

The demons—and their shapes that told of ancient fears—had gone; the green light had turned red. The music had changed too—gone was that maddening, warped guitar lick and in its place, a gentle Bossa Nova beat at a normal pitch and tempo. In any other situation, he would have wiggled his hips to the catchy, familiar rhythm, unable to stop himself from moving with the groove. But this was far, far from normal so he stayed still, deeply suspicious and full of panic as to what might appear next.

The sobbing remained.

Then, entering from stage left, was a new silhouette. It was a woman, a dancing woman. Not just dancing—it was a striptease. On the side of the thin curtain, an exotic dancer was sauntering seductively towards him. What normally might have been a thrill terrified him more than anything had before. His mouth went dry, his stomach churned, and his genitals tingled not in excitement, but in pure fear.

While her shadow suggested a woman of beauty,

his soul was screaming that, if she got to the curtain and pulled it back, what he would see would send him crazy. There was no reason at all for him to think this, yet he knew. He *knew*.

That curtain was, right now, the only thing keeping him sane.

He squeezed on the paper clip until it ripped into his palm, drawing blood.

Nothing happened.

The exotic dancer edged closer and closer to his curtain, eventually reaching up to grab it. Her thin, delicate fingers slowly curled around the edge of the material that had been shutting him off from whatever reality was hiding behind it. Each fingernail on her hand was a different shade of purple; the middle one even had some glitter mixed in, giving it a rather glamorous sparkle.

He clamped his eyes shut and braced himself as the curtain was drawn back in one swift, well-practised swish.

"Oh goodness, you're bleeding. Let me clean that up."

He opened his eyes.

Everything was normal.

Well, apart from being in hospital. But it was

a normal hospital. The sobbing continued, but there were no weird lights, no awful music, and no exotic dancer—just a friendly nurse. She was about his age, slim, and pretty in spite of being bright red in the face from stress, exhaustion, and this damned summer scorcher.

"Apologies that I didn't respond to your call button sooner—it's been one of those days! Everyone's suffering with this heat. It's always the same when it gets like this; the sun gets fired up and we are swamped. Good thing we only get them like this a couple of days a year!"

She smiled. It was a good smile, a *normal* smile. A bonus anchor to the one covered in blood in his palm.

"Sorry—I'm babbling, aren't I? Your tests have all come back clear so you're good to go home as soon as you're ready; let me just clean up this hand first. I tucked your shoes under the bed, by the way."

She reached for the paper clip, meaning to take it off him, and he thought that when she did, he'd be plunged back into that nightmare world, this nice nurse reverting to that sinister dancer. In fact, the more he looked at her, the more he saw that demonic woman from the other side of the veil. Remove the blue uniform, and the nurse's silhouette would match the dancer's perfectly.

It was her! It was the same woman! And she knew why he was holding the paper clip! The moment she took his anchor from him, it would be game over!

But it wasn't. She took the paper clip, and nothing changed. He sighed. It was going to be OK.

Except one thing still bugged him. The sobbing. It hadn't decreased in volume, and it rattled his nerves knowing someone could be in that much pain.

"Nurse, where is that sobbing coming from? Whoever they are, they sound really upset."

The nurse paused from cleaning his hand, looked into his eyes, and frowned.

"Sobbing? There's no one sobbing here."

She pulled back his curtain to show him the rest of the ward. He was the only person in it.

She frowned. "This ward was empty until you arrived. I'd forgotten you were here, to be honest, it's been so quiet."

She was right; no one was sobbing...it had stopped. But the moment the nurse left he knew it would start again. Which, of course, it did.

After she left, the man calmly got off the bed, put on his shoes and prepared to leave, but not before taking his paper clip from the side table where the nurse had dropped it and wrapping his bandaged hand around it. It didn't stop the sobbing, but at least he had his anchor again.

He left the ward, walking down the long, sterile corridors of the hospital. He didn't see anyone else.

The entrance was a huge, ornate door and he pushed it open, stepping back into the sweltering July sunshine, which hadn't calmed down in the slightest while he was inside. He felt a slight tingling in his bandaged hand and a slight tugging at the back of his mind; had he seen something he wasn't supposed to?

Nonetheless, he was happy. His anchor was still tucked into his hand.

Folding his suit jacket over his arm, he began the slow walk home, drinking in the heat of that weird day, heat that continued to radiate off the pavement right up into his face until long after sunset.

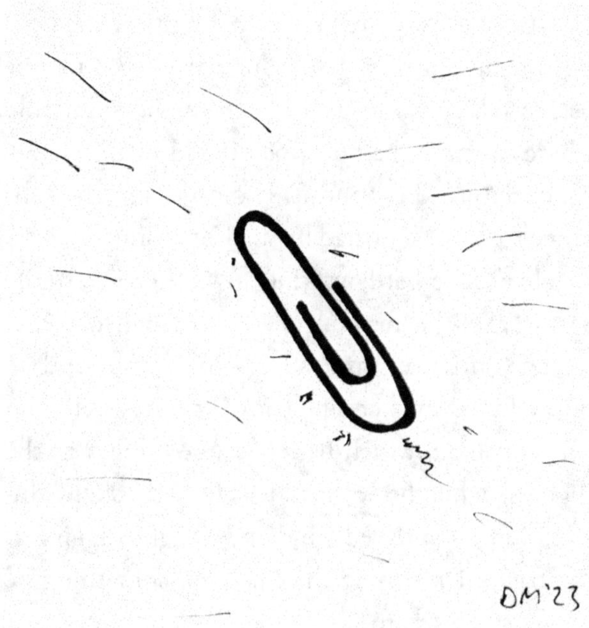

In Too Deep

Charlie let their gaze float over the vast blue ocean as it gently undulated beneath the scorching August sunshine and had one clear thought.

How the hell did I get into this?

It was crazy for them to even be here—hundreds of miles from their very land-locked Warwickshire home in Kingsworth. Just looking at a *picture* of an ocean gave Charlie a mild panic attack—their brain immediately tripped itself up by trying to comprehend the sheer vastness of that body of water, before going down rabbit holes of the unknown: undiscovered monsters that might be lurking underneath and the nowhere-to-go-ness when it came to options for escape if something went wrong.

In short, Charlie and deep water did not mix. Thalassophobia was the proper name for it. Charlie knew this because their brother had looked it up on Wikipedia and WhatsApped them the link, but that knowledge didn't help.

Charlie still couldn't bear the idea of large bodies of mysterious water; the possibility of suffering a slow, sinking death in the deep was just too much. So for Charlie to now be sitting on the edge of a tiny boat—boldly called the *Aquarius*—in full diving gear, ready to flop backwards from their bobbing sanctuary and into the great watery unknown was, if nothing else, an unexpected development.

Deep down Charlie knew this was about facing their fear head on: that damned thalassophobia. But rather than trying less daunting routes like videos, virtual reality, or even just paddling on the beach (even that most basic and gentle life experience had, up until now, been too much to bear), Charlie had decided to dive in.

To their left, Charlie could hear the calming voice of Dean, the instructor for this course, who had been with them from the start, and as soon as all his pupils were underwater, would be right there with them until the end. That voice stopped Charlie woolgathering and tugged them back to the here and now, like being delicately stirred from a deep sleep by a gentle parent.

Back on land, Dean had been kind, friendly, and patient with Charlie, sensing their fear and helping them approach it as best they could. Dean had seen it all before, and was able to use his experience to first convince Charlie to return for the second training session, then keep coming back for further classes, and finally get themselves on this boat, ready to graduate head first into the deep blue.

Charlie glanced over at the instructor to confirm he was definitely there. He was, a huge smile on his face and his personalised lime green mask and mouthpiece hanging around his neck.

Got this custom made from the manufacturer's head office, he'd told Charlie and the rest of the course participants during their second session together, *so you'll always know it's me.*

There was a splash from farther down the *Aquarius* as someone took the plunge, and then Dean squatted in front of Charlie. He raised his eyebrows, silently asking if they were good to go.

Despite the screaming in their brain, Charlie nodded, their heart pounding.

The person immediately to Charlie's left flung themself back into the ocean. Charlie was next. Their chest felt fit to burst, such was the ferocity of their most vital organ's thumping.

Charlie closed their eyes and took a deep breath—inhale for a count of four, exhale for a count of eight. It helped. They did it again, the finger and thumb of their right hand unconsciously grabbing their left ring finger and twirling the gold band they wore. Their grandad's lucky ring—another device Charlie jumped to when in need of some self-soothing.

Touching the ring also helped. Charlie opened their eyes and looked at Dean's understanding face.

Dean smiled, a genuine grin that spread wide and made the corners of his eyes crease in on themselves. "This is it, Charlie. This is your time. You can do it!"

Dean reached out and patted Charlie's left shoulder. As he did, he grimaced and pulled his hand away, squinting at his palm.

"Chewing gum," he said, making a face at the sticky blob that was now in his hand. "I'll make sure these suits get cleaned properly next time. Sorry about that!"

The diver on Charlie's right sneezed with such volume it was like a gunshot. Charlie jumped and their grandad's ring flew out of their hand. It bounced, bobbing towards the edge of the boat, before Dean's hand flashed forward.

SLAM!

He grinned. "That was lucky! Good job that chewing gum was there after all!"

Dean prized the ring out of the secondhand gum and handed it back to Charlie, then asked again if they were good to go. Charlie replaced the ring and gave a firm, confident nod. They counted to three, then pushed backwards into the ocean.

Charlie opened their eyes and could see nothing save for the bubbles their impact had caused. Charlie held their breath and reminded themself that it would clear in a moment—that this was no cause for panic—and their eagerness to believe that was enough to keep Charlie in control. The bubbles went away and the ocean around Charlie calmed.

The view was unlike nothing they'd ever seen before: blue, getting darker and darker, and not much else, except for glimpses of the other student divers on this expedition. It was vaster than Charlie had ever imagined from on land—there was no word to describe its size, its scope, its infinite multitudes ... or how small, powerless, and insignificant Charlie felt now that they were in it. They sensed those ingrained fears bubbling up once again.

Charlie closed their eyes and took another meditative breath: in for four, out for eight. Again, it helped. Charlie opened their eyes just in time to see the edge of something darting towards them.

Charlie's body jerked in surprise and they flailed left, full of panic once more as they tried to evade whatever mystery of the deep had targeted them.

It was only when they moved that they realised there was nothing to fear—it was Dean. Kind and understanding Dean following the rest of the group down into the deep with his distinctive lime green equipment.

So you'll always know it's me.

Dean stopped swimming, put his right hand on Charlie's arm, and used his left to make a circle with his finger and thumb.

You OK, Charlie?

Relieved, Charlie nodded and gave Dean the

double thumbs up. Dean gave them back, then tapped his own chest before pointing down, pointing at Charlie, and pointing down again.

I'm catching those guys up. See you down there.

Another double thumbs up from Charlie was enough for Dean to set off again. Charlie's arms and legs tingled with nerves as they watched the instructor swim out of view. They were wobbling again, those old fears creeping back.

But after a few more deep breaths, those crippling nerves fizzled out. Charlie was strangely calm, finally able to kick their legs and propel themself deeper into the ocean, following Dean and the others.

What was staggering was just how quickly visibility shut down. The water here was so thick, Charlie couldn't see their coursemates' head torches anymore. There was just the occasional ripple.

Then, nothing.

Charlie was alone. Alone in the deep, dark ocean, where anything might be lurking, and—whisper it—they were starting to like it.

They kicked on and went deeper still into the darkness. It was more beautiful and serene than Charlie could have ever imagined. And, more than anything, they were *doing it*. Fuck the panic attacks, fuck the fear, and fuck everything else associated to thalassophobia. Charlie was swimming in the deep blue ocean, and they'd never felt more relaxed.

All those feelings of calm beat a hasty retreat when a shape moved over Charlie, temporarily casting a shadow over them that was noticeable even in those dark waters.

What was that?

The shape passed quickly—there was nothing there when Charlie looked up—but those edgy feelings refused to budge.

Something strong caused the waters around Charlie's right side to move. They peered into the gloom and saw nothing. But they definitely *felt* something. Then, passing underneath, a firm tug, as if they were caught in the slipstream of something. Charlie remained still and tried to breathe.

After that, it all happened quickly.

Something dark and unfathomably large darted in front of Charlie a few yards ahead. It whizzed past too quickly for Charlie to properly make out anything, save for enough pointed shapes to make them think of a certain classic movie with a certain iconic theme tune.

Whatever it was had gone.

In its wake, a diver without a head.

Charlie gasped and turned away only to be greeted with worse: a collection of arms and legs floating behind them. The water was slowly turning a cloudy mixture of crimson and maroon, while bits of gristle and ligaments flicked off the parts they used to be attached to.

Another slipstream brushed past Charlie, who was for a moment unable to move. They eventually found the willpower to slowly turn their gaze, and instantly wished they hadn't. Staring back at them was Dean's head. Charlie knew it was him because of his custom-made lime green mask and matching mouthpiece, which—like the whole head—was no longer connected to anything.

So you'll always know it's me.

That was when Charlie switched into survival mode, with the throb of their heartbeat painful in their ears.

Through a lifetime of suffering from thalassophobia, Charlie had often pictured this moment: an underwater fight or flight scenario. In those daydreams, they'd always picked flight and things had always happened quickly. Faced with it in real life, though, it was like Charlie was living at half-speed.

Charlie's first kick for the surface felt heavy and sluggish—like they were trying to move through treacle and they'd forgotten the most basic motor skill of simply kicking. The water seemed to be working against them in every direction, pushing them back, fixing them in place. Their second kick was a little stronger, but was accompanied by a tingling sensation that rose through the lower half of their body, then through their gut and up to their throat. Charlie finally understood the idea of your heart being in your mouth.

Their third kick was scruffy; Charlie's left flipper caught the back of their right calf and lost all momentum. They began hyperventilating without realising it—sucking oxygen with the force of a vacuum cleaner— disoriented in the great sameness of the oppressive ocean waters.

Kick four was the first, and only one that felt normal, that felt right.

Five kicks in, something felt different to Charlie.

At first, they had no idea what it was, then

it dawned on them: breathable air, or lack of it. Nothing was coming out of their mouthpiece—it had failed when they needed it most. Then, as their panic was really ramping up, the shape appeared over Charlie again. This time, it stopped. It had seen them.

Charlie found themself in a shadow that grew larger as the creature grew closer. Out of the gloom, ghastly details slowly became clear to Charlie.

The huge fin sitting atop a powerful body—a vessel that was the deathly dark grey that had long haunted Charlie's nightmares.

That gunmetal shape, with a smattering of old battle scars on the top two-thirds. Gills that looked like they'd been carved into its body with a rusty, jagged sword, just before its pectoral fin. A dirty white belly underneath. Charlie looked to its pointy head and saw its snout, two dull buttons of onyx for eyes, and teeth.

So many sharp teeth.

This beast of the deep gave its tail a gentle flick and pushed itself towards Charlie, opening its mouth wider and wider as it got closer. Charlie knew this was it. They closed their eyes and—

SLAM!

With a jolt, Charlie looked around. They were back on the *Aquarius*, sitting on its edge in full diving gear, ready to flop backwards into the great watery unknown. Dean had his hand planted palm down on the bench and the person to Charlie's right was wiping their nose on their sleeve.

"That was lucky!" Dean grinned.

"Good job that chewing gum was there after all," Charlie cut in, their voice lacking any enthusiasm.

"You took the words out of my mouth!" said Dean as he handed the ring back to Charlie. "You good to go?"

Without thinking, Charlie nodded, just as the person next to them flung themself into the ocean. Charlie was next. Whatever they'd just seen hadn't happened; it had just been an incredibly vivid daydream.

What if it was more than that? part of Charlie's brain asked, but it didn't receive an answer. It was just that damned thalassophobia trying to win again, and Charlie was determined to stop that from happening.

They looked down at the ocean and, for a moment, thought they saw a shape—a huge looming shape—pass beneath them, but quickly wrote it off as their brain over-complicating things again. This was it. This was Charlie's time. They were going to *do* this!

Charlie counted to three, then pushed backwards into the ocean.

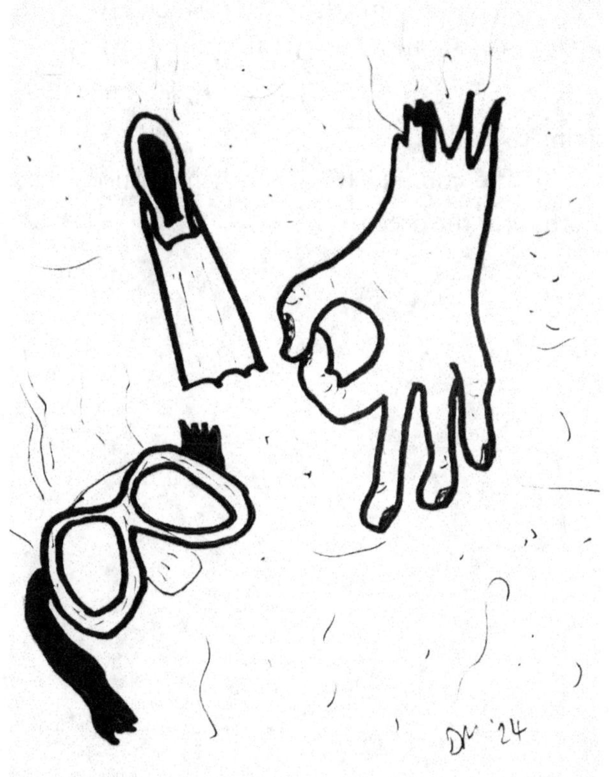

Here's Lookin' At You

"If there's anything else I can do for you during your stay with us, Miss Du Vries," the hotel manager said in that nasally voice she'd hated from the moment she arrived at reception and he had realised who she was—the famous writer staying in this humble little place, "please don't hesitate to ask. If you dial #19, it will come directly to me."

I'd like you to fuck the fuck off. Take *your crooked, coffee-stained teeth, that wafer-thin excuse for a moustache, and your oily, slicked-back hair as far away from me as possible,* Clara thought.

But her PR training kicked in like a reflex and what she actually said was somewhat less hostile.

"That's very kind, thank you. I think I'm all set for the time being. I'm going to take an hour or so to unpack and get my bearings, then I might venture into town. I've never been to Kingsworth before.

"Excellent, excellent—and thank you for choosing us over the big hotel at the top of the High Street. Your custom is very greatly appreciated for an independent little place like ours," the manager said and started edging towards the door, before stopping again.

This is where he'll ask for a photo, or to sign something, she thought. *This is where he asks for a little piece of me to keep forever.*

"I've just realised, I haven't mentioned the painting—silly of me!"

He pointed to the portrait hanging above her bed. It was an oil painting of a middle-aged man dressed entirely in black. He had a full, bushy beard the colour of autumn foliage below a totally bald dome—almost like his head was upside down —and he wore a neutral expression, not even the hint of a smile. He held a single red apple, which complemented his intense, green eyes. The painting was far from beautiful—heck, it wasn't even that good—but it was certainly striking in its bizarreness.

"Leo Harlow, who built this hotel in 1864," the manager explained. "Unfortunately, he died in this very room after eating a poisoned apple—ironic, given how he'd posed for this portrait sitting a few weeks earlier. Maybe the artist killed him—ha!"

The manager smiled in a way that showed too many teeth. It was not a pleasant sight.

Clara frowned as she looked more closely at the portrait. It was doing that thing creepy old paintings tend to do—looking right at her. She knew its eyes would follow her around the room regardless of where she might be standing.

Here's lookin' at you, she thought.

"I know it's a little ... macabre," the manager said with just the slightest chuckle in his voice, "but I thought, given your chosen genre, it might appeal to you. Who knows? Maybe it could be part of your next book!"

He chuckled again, splaying both hands out as wide as they would go—something he didn't even seem to realise he was doing. It was odd.

"Thank you," Clara said. She wanted the manager to leave even more than ever. "It's certainly intriguing... I'll be sure to let you know if inspiration strikes!"

"Excellent. Well, I'll leave you to it—again, dial #19 if you need me."

He finally left.

The moment the door closed behind him and the handle clicked into place, locking the room to anyone outside, Clara lay back on the bed and sighed. She thought about how terrible the manager's attempt at facial hair was and giggled. The giggle soon became proper laughter, and Clara had to roll over and bury her face in the pillow to mute the sound of it, just in case he happened to still be within earshot. He certainly looked like the sort to linger outside, perhaps with one of those ugly, angular ears pressed against the thick wooden door. That image set her laughing even harder.

What stopped her was the sound of a gentle thud as something hit the carpet. Clara looked across the room and saw what had caused it—a red apple, just like the one in the painting.

She looked up at Harlow's portrait and, sure enough, he was staring at her, apple in hand. She didn't remember clocking an apple with the usual tea and coffee provisions when she'd first come into the room, but she'd probably just missed it; she'd had a long journey here after all. It seemed to be the more time you spent in bland, budget-friendly hotels, the fewer details you took in while you were there—which seemed criminal for a fiction writer, really.

Still, it left her feeling ... unnerved. She picked up the apple and placed it next to the kettle in a bowl full of teabags, small tubes of instant coffee, and sugar sachets. It wouldn't be able to roll onto the floor from there.

Clara then slipped into the ensuite to splash some water on her face. It was cold and refreshing. It felt good.

She dried herself with a clean hand towel, then glanced at her reflection in the mirror and jumped. Harlow's face was behind her, staring her right in the eyes again—just like those old portraits always do.

"Give it a rest, Mr. Harlow," Clara said, then returned to the main part of the room and sat down at the small desk by the window. She flipped open her laptop, connected to the surprisingly fast hotel Wi-Fi, and Googled some places where she might eat later, as well as if there was anywhere nice for a short walk. September had done its usual trick of bringing better weather than any of the summer months had been able to offer, and she wanted to make the most of the balmy evening.

A few moments later, just as she was reading the menu of a vegetarian restaurant that came very highly reviewed on TripAdvisor and a walk that was clearly well-loved but that quite possibly had the worst-written directions she'd ever read, Clara paused, feeling like she was being watched. She looked slightly to her left and almost screamed when she saw Harlow's face staring at her from a different framed picture on the wall.

Get a grip, Clara told herself. *It's just a reflection.*

Which, of course, it was—even if it was so clear that it was as though Harlow had actually moved to that other picture, a photo of Kingsworth's high street from the 1930s. It was scarily clear, in fact.

Clara looked back at the portrait and there it was, just as before, staring back at her, Harlow still holding his apple and looking a little bored. She decided that some fresh air before dinner would definitely be a good move—terrible directions be damned—and went over to the wardrobe where the hotel manager had stowed her suitcase and hung her jacket.

She opened the door and again stifled a scream

when Harlow's face appeared in the thin mirror on the inside of the cupboard door.

Another reflection, she told herself, heart racing, *just another reflection. Kind of surprising that there's one here, as the angles don't look like they would match up. But hey, what do I know? I'm a writer, not a scientist.*

She pulled on the jacket even though it was probably warm enough outside for her not to bother with it, shut the wardrobe, turned around to grab her purse, then stopped dead.

The apple was on the floor again. She also had that prickly feeling of being watched—which, of course, she was. Clara glanced at Harlow's portrait again and saw it looking back at her, apple still in hand.

"You're messing with my head, Leo. If I promise to write about you in my next book, will you back off a bit?"

The painting didn't react, naturally—it was just a painting after all—but Clara could have sworn she felt something in the air, a kind of throb or a hum.

She replaced the apple, picked up her purse,

and strode to the door. She gripped the handle, pulled it down, and ... nothing.

It wouldn't open.

She was locked inside.

"Fuck's sake," Clara said, trying it again a few more times just to be sure. It didn't budge.

Letting out a frustrated sigh, she threw her purse on the bed and grabbed the phone off the side table. She punched #19 and listened as the line started to blip, kind of like those little beeps they play on Radio 4 at the top of the hour.

She looked up again at Leo Harlow's portrait. He stared back at her.

"Look," she said, "you're in, OK? I will *definitely* put you in my new book, but I can't write on an empty stomach and this stuffy room is giving me a headache. So if you're holding the door, how about letting it go? We've got all night to hang out."

Harlow didn't react, but there was a different look and feel about the picture. Clara couldn't quite pinpoint what, but it was ... something.

The phone continued to gently blip as she waited for the manager to pick up, but in between those small sounds, she heard another one in her room. A thud.

Clara looked up. The apple was back on the floor.

It was only now, as she held the phone to her ear waiting for that hopeless manager to answer, that she noticed how many pictures dotted the room. Each wall had half a dozen, at least—photos, drawings, paintings—and in every one, she saw Harlow's reflection watching her.

At least, she assumed it was his reflection, even though it did look like it was actually him in every single one.

Just as her heartbeat was starting to get so strong she could feel it in her temple, the blips on the phone stopped, and Clara heard someone pick up.

"Hello? It's Clara Du Vries. Something is wrong with my door. I can't open it and I'd like to head into town, so I wondered if you could send some-one to—"

"Eat the apple, Miss Du Vries," said a voice that wasn't that of the hotel manager.

Clara swallowed and quickly scanned the room, taking in all the Leo Harlows staring at her from every wall. They couldn't all be reflections, surely? So many faces, so many eyes, boring into her from every angle. It was intense.

"Eat the apple and everything will be fine," the voice said before cutting the call.

Clara dropped the phone on the bed. As she stared at the handset, now lying askew and out of place on her pillow, she heard a series of noises.

Thud.

Thud.

Thud, thud.

Th-th-th-thud-d-d-d.

She slowly, painfully turned around, already knowing what she would see: apples. Dozens of apples. A whole tree's worth had seemingly dropped from nothing onto the carpet of this miserable hotel room. Some were motionless; others were still bobbing and steadying themselves after their landing.

All of them were red.

She turned her head and looked back at Leo Harlow's portrait, only then realising what was different.

He wasn't holding an apple any more. Unlike before, his hands were empty, and that neutral expression he'd been wearing had vanished too. Now, he was smiling.

Dear God, he was smiling!

Halloween Special—The Hunt for Rupi-K

"How much farther is it, Jake?" asked Felix. "Much as I appreciate all these trees and their autumn colours, I'd rather just get this fucking thing filmed."

Jake smirked without looking back at his friend.

"Why's that? Scared?"

"No," Felix replied. "I'm just buzzed for Justine's Halloween party tonight. She and I have ... plans."

"Well, bully for you," said Gregory from off to the right, taking a final drag on his almost-spent cigarette.

"Bully for him? What does that mean?" Logan asked, two steps behind them.

"No idea." Gregory shrugged. "I read it some-where."

"Of course you did. Bully for you," sneered Felix.

Gregory didn't reply with words—his raised middle finger did all of the talking necessary.

The foursome were walking down a straight, wide path with a smattering of trees on one side and a farmer's field on the other. All of them had a camera in their hand or slung over their shoulders, not to capture the late October scenery, but for videoing.

Together, they were the team behind Fork_Boys, a YouTube channel they'd started eighteen months earlier and which had, to their surprise, gone viral. A significant number of people seemed to enjoy seeing four spoiled, privileged, and annoying white teenage boys smoking, climbing things, and generally bullshitting on screen multiple times a week.

Today, they were filming their Halloween special.

"Seriously though, Jake, how much farther?" Logan chipped in.

Jake barely looked up from his phone. "It's not

far. There's a footbridge just up ahead and it's on the other side."

They carried on with little chat. They all had their minds on other things: tonight's party, girls, tomorrow's edit of the footage that they were about to gather, girls, their ever-growing legend and bank balances, and well, girls, again.

Fork_Boys had been birthed out of boredom. One weekend, three of them had been together at Gregory's house doing little of importance, when Jake arrived toting a new camera and suggested they make a stupid video just for something to do.

An hour later, Jake had more footage of the other three lighting their farts, whipping each other with wet tea towels, and drinking shots of hot sauce than he knew what to do with, but they used Gregory's laptop to snip something together. They created the channel there and then—Felix came up with the delightful name—hit upload, and didn't think much more of it.

Then the views started coming in, so they made more videos. After that, it became a habit.

Now, making the videos was still fun, but it had become more of a chore than it used to be. Still, the social status—and the money—was worth it.

The footpath narrowed as it curved to the right, following the edge of the field. The trees on the left ended as the verge dropped down sharply, and the sound of traffic roared into their ears, as if it had been switched on from a hidden speaker.

"Here we go," said Jake.

Ahead of them was a footbridge, about two metres wide, that stretched over the dual carriageway before plunging down towards a canopy of red, orange, yellow, and brown.

"Let me just get some scenery shots," said Gregory, already holding his camera up to his face. "You pricks never give me anything good to put the titles over."

While Gregory's camera whirred, the other three lit cigarettes. Each watching the Saturday afternoon traffic whiz underneath them.

"It's closer to the road than I'd thought," Logan mused. "Like, it's literally right next to it. Feels weird to think what happened there was so near to such a big road. You'd think someone would have seen something."

"Yeah, I guess, but it's not exactly easy access, is it?" said Felix.

As usual, they all dropped their spent cigarette

butts without a shred of remorse for their collective act of littering, before crossing the bridge.

As soon as they hit the other side, everything grew darker. The trees here were much thicker, and even though they could clearly hear the road that was only metres away, they couldn't see it.

They also couldn't be seen from the outside.

"Come on. I'm bored of waiting." Jake led them forward.

The path swung round to the left and revealed what they'd trekked here for: the entrance to Gage Woods, a beautiful slice of nature with a dark secret.

The woods defied logic; they were huge, yet you couldn't appreciate their full size until you were up close—the same idiom about wood and trees was tapping at the skulls of each of the boys, but it was so obvious none of them let it in or gave it a voice. Their minds were elsewhere, unaware of just how foreboding such a mass of trees were, nor who or what might be in there watching them from some hidden place.

"Who's doing the intro?" asked Logan. "I've lost track of whose turn it is."

"It's me," said Felix. "Let's do it up there where the path splits."

Although none of the four boys would admit it out loud, there was something spooky about these woods. The trees were tall, with thick trunks, and they didn't quite grow straight. They leaned in slightly as they got closer to the clouds, giving the impression of looming over whoever dared to walk under them. They blocked those souls from the view of anyone else.

It wasn't just the huge trees. The woods were quiet, eerily so. Even the noise of the road had already been dampened to a murmur. They were a twenty-minute walk away from their own parked car, but might as well have been in another world.

They headed towards the split in the path, blissfully ignorant of the fact that they were being watched.

As they got closer to the junction, they noticed something fixed to the tree around which the path split. The thing was a piece of wood— rectangular, about the size of a postcard, and it had once been white but was now battered by the weather, making it dull grey.

It was a sign, nailed to the tree trunk. Most

of the sign was filled by four chunky black arrows pointing in different directions. It was only when they got close enough to run their hands over its rough surface that they saw what was written on it.

BEGIN was written in the middle of the arrows in dark blood-red, scrawled by a hand that could have been that of a child or an unhinged adult.

Logan already had his camera out to capture it. He looked at Felix, raised his eyebrows, and nodded.

You're up.

Felix smoothed out the sleeves of his denim shirt, wiped the lenses of his glasses, then spat to one side. Logan settled the camera square on him, while Gregory and Jake started rolling to gather their trademark quirky side shots.

They were ready.

"Welcome, Forkers!" Felix beamed in his best YouTuber voice. "Welcome, all, to episode 289—our Halloween special! To all our fantastic sub-scribers—thanks for coming back—and if you've not hit that button yet ... what are you waiting for?"

He dropped back to his usual, boring, voice.

"You'll be adding something cheesy and campy there, right, Gregory? Dripping gore or some shit?"

Gregory nodded and twirled his hand.

Keep going.

Felix switched back to presenter mode. "For this spooky special, we've come to the legendary Gage Woods, which are just outside our home-town of Kingsworth. This used to be a happy place, a charming little set of woods, where a bunch of well-meaning adults built four different assault courses for kids to run through."

He paused for effect.

"But nineteen years ago, on Halloween, every-thing changed. That was when *she* went missing—Rupinder Kaur. Rupi-K to her friends."

Another brief pause.

"She and three of her mates had come to run around the course, just as they'd done loads of times before. Only this time, Rupi-K never came back. They searched these woods for days and never discovered what happened to her. But they knew *something* had happened to poor Rupi-K—something *awful*."

He stepped aside to point at the sign nailed to the tree.

"On each of these four paths, they found a different piece of Rupi-K."

Felix counted with his fingers.

"First, the lower part of her left leg, still with her white Reebok classic trainer on the foot. Second, her right ring finger, her brown skin set off with the purple nail polish she'd used that morning. Third, her left ear. Last, most gruesome of all, her right eye."

Felix screwed up his face into an expression of disgust.

"Now, this Halloween, your favourite Fork Boys are going to take one path each and see if we can find out what happened to Rupi-K. And if we can't, well … you know what else we like to do."

Felix smiled his sick, slightly-mad-looking grin that he'd developed specifically for YouTube, holding it for far longer than necessary.

Logan flipped the screen of his camera closed. "OK, done. You can stop staring at me like a fucking psycho now."

"Why's that?" Felix smirked. "Scared?"

"No. It just makes you look even uglier than usual."

The boys all laughed at that well-worn bit of

banter. It was a good sound, a normal sound, and one that disguised what they were all actually now feeling somewhere inside those thick skulls of theirs.

"OK," said Jake, "everyone ready?"

The others nodded.

"I'll take that one," he pointed to the path on the far left, "you take the next one, Gregory, then Logan, and Felix takes the far right. From what I read online, each course should bring us right back here and only takes about fifteen minutes, so we can meet back here and be done with it."

Jake switched his camera on and started down his path.

"Just remember, keep recording the whole time. And if you see Rupi-K, I don't know ... scream?"

He laughed as he walked away.

Each boy set off down their paths. Within a few metres, they were lost to the thick autumnal foliage and darkness beyond it. The woods swallowed them.

What had been watching the boys waited a moment, then stepped forwards. It looked across the four paths, picked one, and followed.

***

Logan stopped mid-sentence to blow cigarette smoke down the lens—his signature move.

"But what Felix didn't mention in his intro was how we're not just here on the off-chance of finding a dead body. Oh, no. Forkers, legend has it Rupi-K is still here, haunting Gage Woods and looking for revenge."

He dodged a low-hanging branch, then took another drag of nicotine.

"You see, the rumours 'round here have always been that what happened to Rupi-K was no accident. Apparently, these woods were also the hangout of a bunch of racist yobs. And, well, when a brown girl walked into their place with no one else around, they went to work ... and went way too far."

Logan flicked his cigarette butt off screen while he continued to address the camera.

"Naturally, the local legend now is that Rupi-K reappears every Halloween, the anniversary of her disappearance, hobbling around and trying to piece her body back together so she can either move onto the next world or hunt down whoever killed her. I'm never really sure on that part, and it's probably all bullshit anyway."

Logan looked up and frowned. Then grinned.

"Ah, looks like we have our first piece of playground equipment—you remember Felix talking about the mini-assault courses, right? Let's have a look."

He panned the camera round, showing the path rising slightly to a crest and then dropping away. To the left was another one of those battered signs. On this one, the camera picked out the words SLIDE-DIE-SLIDE, the middle word printed in the same blood-red as earlier.

"Slidey slide," Logan read. "Cute—I guess we've got ourselves a slide!"

He climbed to the top, then filmed the view ahead of him. It was a fairly short but steep descent to what looked like a soft clearing of springy moss below. The route from top to bottom? A rough-and-ready slide made out pieces of well-sanded plywood.

Logan turned the camera back to his face and grinned again.

"Here we go, Forkers!" he shouted, and pushed off.

Should anyone ever stumble across the memory card with Logan's footage, they would be able to pinpoint the moment it happened. His eyes widened, he shouted out in genuine pain, then flailed over to one side before landing at the bottom with a thud, his camera rolling away from him.

"Shit! Shit! Shit!" he yelped before picking up his camera. A gush of red liquid flowed down the lens as he manoeuvred it round so he was facing it once more. There were tears in his eyes.

"Oh FUCK, that hurts!" he grimaced. "My hand went over something sharp on the way down and I think I've cut my finger badly. I'm bleeding everywhere."

He held his right hand up to his face. Something was missing.

Where his ring finger should have been was now just a stump spurting blood. When Logan's brain finally registered what had happened, he did the obvious thing.

He screamed.

And he didn't stop filming. Even facing life as some sort of deformed thing, part of his brain knew what *incredible* content this was.

He was so engrossed in his mixture of anguish

and imagined royalties he didn't notice what was creeping up behind. His camera saw it, though: a cloaked figure limping towards him.

Logan let his tears continue to fall as he tried to come up with some witty line on the fly, while also mentally trying to work out what in the fuck he could do to stop the bleeding. Could you die from a severed finger?

He finally stemmed his tears, steadied himself, and looked at the camera, mouth open and ready to speak.

That was when it made its move. A hand came around the right side of Logan's face and clamped over his mouth. He had just enough time to notice the brown skin, the purple nails, and the fact that it was missing the same finger he'd just lost, before a flash of something sharp-looking swept in front of his eyes from left to right and then under his chin.

There was no real pain this time, just a sudden feeling of wet warmth leaking from his neck. He looked down at his camera; the lens was covered in blood. It dropped from his hands and hit the ground.

Logan gurgled something that sounded like the letter *k*, then flopped forwards.

His camera was still rolling, but it wouldn't be for much longer. A pair of blood-soaked hands picked it up, carried it a few steps to the side and then pointed the lens at a large rock on the ground. It quickly got even larger in the frame as man-made technology rushed to meet that which was from the earth. There was a loud crack, followed by a crunch, and a scar of pure, white light slashed across the screen.

Then: black.

***

Felix focused his camera on the sign nailed to the tree. It was just like the others, only this one said SWING DING A-LING. He then slowly panned to the left and upwards, to take in the rustic swing—a plank of battered wood sitting across a loop of faded blue rope that hung from a high branch.

The swing was high, the seat resting about five feet off the ground. To help reach it, more scraps of wood had been nailed to the tree trunk as a makeshift ladder.

The camera jerked and wobbled before finally

settling as Felix set it on the ground and framed the swing.

Once that was done, he squatted in front of the lens. He was just about to speak when a scream pierced the air.

Felix chuckled. "Ah, Logan.. thinks he's so original."

Felix absent-mindedly wiped his mouth with the back of his hand, then stared back down the lens. "Ignore that blonde idiot; he's just trying to freak us out. Now, where was I before we found this swing?"

He wiped his mouth again.

"Oh yeah, the question of whether it's the ghost of Rupi-K who lives in these woods or Rupi-K herself. The thing is, no one can say for sure, can they? They never found her body—just those four parts I told you about earlier."

He paused again, this time to push his glasses back up his nose.

"It's hard to think that she could still actually be in these woods—not with those injuries—but I guess you never know. Personally, I think—"

From somewhere in the near distance came a loud crack, like a twig being stepped on. Felix looked around on both sides, then diverted his eyes back to his camera and smiled.

"That, Forkers, is almost certainly Logan trying to freak me out some more. What a twat ... but a good enough reason for me to get on this swing, I guess. Leave your scores for my dismount in the comments!"

Felix stood up so that only his feet filled the frame. As he walked towards the swing, more of him came into view. He climbed the nailed-on ladder with relative ease and managed to pull the swing close enough to stand on with both feet, while still gripping the tree with one hand.

"Here we go!" he shouted, and pushed off from the trunk.

Almost immediately, the wood on the swing snapped, and Felix dropped straight down. He would have fallen but for his arms, which got caught in the rope and left him hanging a few inches above the ground.

Had Felix been a little taller, his feet would have landed back on the earth and he could have easily disentangled himself. As it was, he was stuck.

Trapped.

"For fuck's sake!" he hissed, struggling to get

untangled. His camera picked up how the rope around him tightened and slowly rotated him in mid-air so he no longer faced the lens.

Suddenly, the view was blocked by something new. A brown-skinned leg that ended in a filthy Reebok classic trainer poked out of muddy blue denim, along with something that looked like a pirate's leg but made out of a branch.

As this new arrival moved away from the camera and towards the prone Felix, it revealed a human shape dressed in a long, dark cloak. Trailing from its left hand was something ragged and sharp, some sort of rustic, handmade weapon—a blade of jagged metal flecked with spots of something rust-coloured that had been roughly tied to a thick, short branch.

Felix was still struggling and cursing, completely unaware of his new scene-mate. His blissful ignorance didn't last long.

The cloaked figure with one shoe and one stump shifted the sharp thing to its right hand, reaching it towards the left side of Felix's head.

Felix's camera couldn't pick out what had happened exactly, but did capture his reaction. He screamed. It was a powerful scream that rippled through the trees and sent birds scattering in all directions. Although, such was the thickness of the woods, it still didn't make it out of the trees.

The traffic travelling on the road bordering Gage Woods zoomed on, unaware.

The figure was using a sawing action down the side of Felix's head. It strained but never faltered, before relaxing and taking a step to the side. Blood poured from Felix's head, the cloaked figure now holding a chunk of flesh in its left hand.

Felix's hanging form spun in an agonisingly slow circle until he was facing his attacker. When he saw what he was looking at, he opened his mouth wide and screamed again.

The figure waited for a moment, then swept the blade down Felix's front, slicing him open from collarbone to groin, before doubling back across his lower torso to spill his guts in an angry, steaming red mess.

Felix flinched a couple more times, then was still.

The figure lurched back towards the camera, stopping right by the lens. It carefully placed Felix's severed ear on the ground. The picture jerked slightly as the camera was picked up and pointed downwards.

The microphone picked up a slight grunt before the frame went black with a clunk.

***

"Pathetic," Gregory spat. "Absolutely pathetic, both of them."

His camera tracked the path in front of him—Gregory was a behind-the-camera guy—but he was happy to commentate as his feet stomped along the zig-zagging track.

"Just because it's a Halloween special, they have to go and scream. Pricks."

The woods were quiet again now though, and Gregory let the next few seconds run on in silence, save for the sounds of his own feet brushing through the undergrowth. Dead leaves crunched beneath his trainers, and every so often a twig would snap with a crisp *pop*.

"I guess I should offer my thoughts on this Rupi-K kid, but I don't really have much to say. I didn't grow up 'round here, didn't even know her story until Jake suggested we do this special. I'm sure the others will have talked about it to death though; you know what they're like."

Gregory followed the path's next kink round to the left, where it became noticeably wider and straighter. And darker. The trees on either side of the path leaned even more obviously into each other here, creating a thick canopy blazing with all the colours of fire, and the picture on Gregory's screen became difficult to make out.

"Interesting," he said, and stopped moving. He adjusted the exposure and the scene came into better focus.

Laid out on the path were two parallel rows of old tyres, the right-hand side slightly nudged forward from the left to create an obvious stepping pattern. On both sides of the tyres, tight against their edges, were masses of twigs and branches, all snapped off in sharp points.

Gregory zoomed in. "Wouldn't want to fall into those. I'm guessing they used to be looked after a little better than that. Back when kids still played here."

By the first tyre was a sign, just like the one back at the start. Like the other, it was nailed to a tree and was written in that crazy writing. HOP-HOP-HOP!

In a rare moment of wanting the spotlight, Gregory turned the camera to his own face.

"Suppose I'd better do this—it is an assault course after all. And, well, you saw how it was set up. If I want to move forwards, it's my only option. If I try going through those branches, I'll end up stuck like a pig."

He smiled. "Wish me luck!"

Before he could move, his eyes widened and he let out a short gasp. He quickly turned the camera back round and zoomed in on what he'd seen.

A deer. A beautiful roe deer casually walked across the path where the rows of tyres ended. It turned towards Gregory and looked down his lens.

"Wow," Gregory whispered, "this is just like that bit in—"

He was interrupted by a swoosh and the deer staggering to one side. An arrow was sticking out of its neck and it was bleeding heavily.

Gregory didn't waste time thinking. He darted forwards, running the assault course as it had been intended. His camera, attached to a strap hung around his neck, bobbed on his left hip.

A few paces in, there was a loud *crack* followed by a shriek from Gregory, who stopped running.

"Oh, Jesus fucking Christ!" he wailed. "HELP!"

He didn't pick up his camera again, but the all-seeing lens caught what had happened anyway. The lower part of his left leg was caught in a rusty bear trap, the teeth of it sinking deep into his flesh. With every movement Gregory made, no matter how small, the trap tore a little deeper, through gristle and sinews and into the bones underneath.

The camera picked up the sound of Gregory vomiting, then crying, before another of those whooshing sounds.

Gregory screamed again as the arrow hit and flailed his arms, but he wasn't able to keep his balance.

He twisted and started to drop to the left. There was a sick ripping as the trap chomped off the part of Gregory's leg it had claimed as its own.

Gravity did the rest for Gregory, who fell into the pile of sharpened sticks. Somehow, his camera spun round enough to capture his final shot, lying on the ground with far less leg than he'd had a few seconds ago, branches piercing his chest and throat.

The camera stayed on Gregory's dying form

for a few moments, before there was yet another whoosh, followed by a thud that knocked it flying.

The screen went black.

***

Jake was frantic, turning in circles and sobbing uncontrollably. But, naturally, still filming.

"Guys, I'm really scared now. That amount of screaming, from all three of them—it can't be one big joke. I really think something bad has happened. I need to look for the others."

He paused to wipe his eyes, then turned his camera round quickly to check something.

"Oh shit, my battery is dying. Look, I'll switch this back on later when I know more. God, I hope they're OK."

Jake stopped recording, replaced the lens cap on his camera, and stopped running.

He stopped crying too. They weren't real tears anyway—it was all part of the plan.

As he sauntered back towards the sign where they'd recorded the intro, Jake fished out a cigarette and lit it. It seemed as though everything had gone to plan. His crazy, selfish, bloodthirsty plan was coming off.

More than any of the others, the dopamine hit of views, comments and subscribers, plus the monetary gain of ad revenue had enthralled Jake. It didn't take long for him to realise he wanted to do this on his own and keep everything for himself. He'd started planting the story of Rupi-K right around the previous Halloween.

The local lore was already there for the others to lose themselves in and while they did, Jake plotted.

It seemed crazy to try and find a hitman to take out the three guys who were supposedly his best friends, but by the time he started hunting around the dark web, sane Jake had left the building.

What was most scary for Jake was not the thought of killing his friends for the sake of You-Tube fame, but more how easy it was to buy death, if you knew where to look.

Jake reached the entrance to the four trails and sat down with his back against a tree trunk. He pulled out his phone, but saw it was still struggling for signal, so he walked a few more steps towards the road, hoping for a few bars, something he hadn't had since they dropped onto this side of the footbridge.

This spot was where he'd arranged to meet Sameer, the guy he hired to do his dirty work, so it made sense to be contactable, especially, as he'd been in a signal dead zone for the last half an hour or so.

As his phone hunted for a signal, Jake heard shuffling behind him. He glanced around and was in no way surprised to see the cloaked figure—one leg ending in a Reebok classic, the other in a crudely-fashioned stump—covered in blood.

"I was just about to call you," Jake said, holding up his phone. "Great job—you've really nailed the look, by the way."

He glanced down at the figure's left hand, which was holding a bundle of bloodied flesh.

Jake was impressed. "Excellent attention to detail with the purple nails, too. I'd forgotten that part myself until Felix mentioned it in the intro."

He nodded at the grim bundle the figure was holding.

"Lay those parts out on the ground. Once I shoot that, we can wrap this up—you can give me the memory cards from the other guys when we get back to the car park."

The figure released its bloody bundle. The severed leg, ear, and finger hit the footpath.

Jake looked at the plunder, then frowned.

"Wait, wait Sameer," he said, squatting to get a better look, "where's the eye? We can't do this without all of the parts. I made that very clear in my confirmation email. Fuck's sake—you're going have to go back to one of them and sort this. Which body is the easiest to get to?"

The cloaked figure did not speak or move. It simply stood facing Jake with its arms folded and face in total darkness.

"Well? What are you waiting for? I've got places to be and a video to edit that will get me what I deserve. Go. Get. A. Fucking. Eye!"

As Jake spat out this order, his phone beeped, then beeped again, then a third time—it had finally found a signal.

Jake looked at the screen. Three messages, all from Sameer.

His heartbeat quickened as he opened them, all sent in quick succession forty minutes earlier, just minutes after he'd dropped out of range.

Jake, there's been a pile-up on the motorway ahead of me and I can't get round it. I've got no chance of making it there on time.

Sorry, man, I was so looking forward to this one—you should see the costume I've made up!

I'll refund the money as soon as I can. Call me if you want to rearrange.

Jake's mouth went dry. Sameer wasn't here, had never been here. Which meant ...

He looked up at the cloaked figure. There was no noise in the woods, save for the murmur of the main road, which sounded much farther away than it actually was.

"What the—" Jake started, when the figure un-folded its arms and let both hands drop free of its cloak sleeves. The right hand was missing a finger. That figure definitely wasn't Sameer—Jake wasn't paying enough for his hitman to permanently dis-figure himself just for one job.

"No," he whispered. "You can't be her."

He made as if to run, but in his confusion and

terror, the message to his feet got scrambled. His legs tangled and he stumbled, then fell.

The cloaked figure closed the distance to Jake with astounding speed. He tried to crawl backwards, but his entire body turned to jelly. His bladder let go, but he barely noticed.

"No, Rupi, no, please ..." he muttered, one hand raised in defence.

Rupi-K paused, her hooded head looking down at Jake like a cat toying with its prey. She tilted her head to one side and stared at him, flexed both her hands, then attacked.

In one swift movement, she raised the sharp branch that sat in the place where her left leg used to be and rammed it through Jake's throat. Jake felt and heard every layer being pierced: the soft skin under his jaw, the hitching cords of his larynx, his spinal column, and then more soft skin at the back as he was pinned to the ground.

Blood gushed out of his neck and Jake gurgled helplessly as the life trickled out of him. Real tears streamed from his eyes now, along with snot from his nose, and his bowels loosened to make even more of a mess downstairs.

Rupi-K twisted her stump a little for an extra

bit of fun, then crouched down close to Jake's face. Before he expired, she reached forward and slowly clawed out one of his eyes. When she wrenched her stump out of him and fixed it back to her leg, he was dead.

She placed Jake's eye with the rest of her afternoon's trophies, the set finally complete. She'd deal with them later—no one ever came to these woods on Halloween weekend after what had happened to her all those years ago.

For now, she had another body and another camera to dispose of. She grabbed Jake's ankles and dragged him back into Gage Woods, ready to reunite the Fork_Boys for one final get-together.

slide
~die~
slide

Spots

*Mid-afternoon, Happy Woodland Nursery
main office*

The shrill warble of the office phone was cut off mid-ring as Emma snatched it from the cradle. Her eyes were wide with panic; she could feel the nervous sweat not only racing down her spine but also dripping from her armpits.

"Laura?" she almost yelled into the handpiece, ignoring all the usual phone-answering protocol. "Laura! Speak to me!"

Emma squinted, trying to hear something positive, but the only sound that came through was a strange static, like the sort that would play from a white noise machine. Only this sound was vicious, jarring, ear-splitting. Underneath that distressing racket, Emma thought she could hear the panicked voices of her colleagues.

Clara rushed over to Emma's desk and mouthed 'speaker' at her. Emma nodded and pushed the button that broadcast the call to the room. Now both women could hear the heinous, fuzzy alien squall.

"Laura!" Emma tried again. "Laura! Matt! Kirsty! Margot!" Her hysteria inched up with each name.

Clara put a hand on Emma's arm to try and comfort her.

"Someone! Anyone! Please answer!" Emma shouted.

In response, the static, but still with undertones of other voices. Then—quiet but unmistakable— came the sound of screaming.

"What was that?" Clara asked, fear etched onto her face. At the same time, there was a loud noise in their office—a *clunk,* as their door locked on its own.

Clara rushed to the door and rattled the handle, but it was no good—it had somehow been locked from the outside. She rushed back to Emma and soon both women were yelling the names of their colleagues over and over into the speaker phone, desperate for someone to pick up.

Finally, someone did. There was a heavy thud followed by a rustle as someone clumsily picked up the other end of the line.

"Laura?" Emma asked, "Laura, is that you?"

It wasn't Laura.

Above the din of the white noise and the continued screaming underneath came the very loud sound of a toddler laughing.

"Ha! HA! HAAH!"

The line went dead.

Emma and Clara looked at each other, both of them failing to find anything to say. Then the office was bleached out in a bright white light and very little mattered anymore.

***

Three hours earlier, Happy Woodland Nursery main office

Clara darted back to the front office when the phone started to ring. She picked up the receiver, cutting off its shrill warble mid-flow.

"Happy Woodland Nursery," she said on auto-pilot in her best customer-facing voice that came naturally after almost 20 years running this delightful daycare, which offered daycare services for equally delightful middle class kids in the obviously delightful middle class haven of Kingsworth. "Clara speaking."

"Hey, Clara, it's Laura," the voice on the other end of the line replied.

"Hello, Laura, love," Clara said to her colleague, smiling as she did. "Is everything OK?"

There was a brief pause as the sound of a toddler screaming with sheer delight ran through the background before Laura spoke again with a mild chuckle.

"Can you send Emma over to the Badger Sett? Something weird is going on with the kids and we're a bit stumped by it."

The Badger Sett was the delightfully cutesy name for the room holding the nursery's second-oldest kids—those who would turn three over the course of that academic year—and Laura was its leader. They were a fun group, old enough to actually do interesting stuff—painting, playing games with something resembling rules and structure, and as had just been evidenced, tanking around with absolute glee. The Badgers were full of beans, sure, but also still young enough to need a nap once a day, giving the staff in there a blessed hour of quiet to grab a cup of tea and let their ears recover a little. That was how it was sold to them anyway—the reality was sixty minutes or so of cleaning, tidying, and paperwork.

Clara frowned. "Of course, Laura. What can I tell her about it?"

Laura made a slight clicking sound, then answered.

"Spots. Two spots have appeared on the face of every child in the room today. Only they don't look like chicken pox or anything along those lines, they're just little red circles—perfect red circles. They're on slightly different parts of their faces, but they definitely all have them."

She paused.

"There's none of these spots on their bodies, their temperatures are all fine, and they otherwise seem totally normal. But ..."

Clara waited for Laura to continue, drawing on her years of experience to know when to stay quiet and let the other person get it all out.

"Well, we'd just like another pair of eyes on them," she finished.

"No problem Laura. I'll send Emma over now. And thanks for calling—you did the right thing."

She replaced the phone and headed back to the kitchen to fill her business partner in on the news.

A few minutes later, Emma was heading across to the Badger Sett. She was always the one to get involved with the kids and go out to any of their four rooms if needed. It's why she and Clara were such a good team; Emma hit the front line, while Clara did all the boring financial and administrative stuff. They were each happy with their lot and, as a result, worked well together.

Emma let out a gasp as a stab of chilly November air whipped around her exposed throat, its icy fingers clawing at her neckline, desperate to be invited in. She zipped her jacket all the way up to her chin, batting away nature's chilly roaming hands.

The Badger Sett was the farthest room from the office, which meant Emma got to the full range of Happy Woodland kids on the walk over. Well, almost. The tiny ones in the baby room wouldn't be outside on a cold day like this, but all the other rooms were letting their residents enjoy some fresh air. That was part of the delightful appeal of this delightful place—outdoor experiences at every opportunity!

Emma passed the Bunny Burrow first, the room that catered to kids too old for the baby room but not ready to become a Badger yet. It was always a hilarious sight—a mixture of walking abilities that had almost two dozen little people staggering and flailing around their Astroturfed garden like they were the world's youngest stag and hen parties out on a big session. Emma laughed and waved as she went past. Some children smiled at her; some looked confused. Most were too busy in their own worlds to even notice.

The vicious November wind whipped and flicked at Emma's cheeks, stinging her nostrils as she rounded the corner of the Bunny Burrow and moved towards the preschoolers. How those little bodies could enjoy being outside when it was this cold, she would never know. Nineteen years of working with kids hadn't explained this resistance to winter to her, and she thought not even another nineteen would either.

The preschoolers were all much more aware of Emma as she passed their garden, and all seemed to have something Very Important to show her. She said she had to go to the Badger Sett first, but promised to stop off on her way back. Being the delightful little middle class kids they were, they all accepted Emma's answer and went back to playing.

Picking up her speed, Emma continued towards the Badger Sett, another jolt of cold wind causing her eyes to water. *Wish I'd put my hat on*, she thought as she finally made it to the little black-and-white gate.

Apart from feeling the cold, there had been nothing on Emma's walk over from the office to give her cause for concern. It was just another normal day full of normal things at the Happy Woodland Nursery. As she walked through the Badger Sett gate, closing it carefully behind her, she hoped it would stay that way.

***

Late morning, the Badger Sett garden

A few minutes later, Emma was just as perplexed as Laura had sounded on the phone.

Every child in the Badger Sett had two little

spots somewhere on their face. Some were on foreheads, some on cheeks, some on necks, but only ever two on each child.

And, just as Laura had said, they didn't look like regular spots. When Emma got close, she could see they were all actually perfectly circular—like tiny stamps—and they seemed to give off a slight but noticeable wave of heat, although they hadn't caused the children to have a fever.

"Talk me through when you noticed them," Emma said. "I really don't think I've ever seen anything like it."

"I know, right?" said Laura. "I'm glad it's not just me who thought they were weird."

Emma grinned as the children ran in all directions across the room, avoiding clattering into her and Laura's legs as if by some unconscious obstacle-sensing safety system.

Zoom! Whiz! Whoosh!

Just as in all the other gardens for all the other rooms, everything seemed normal here. The kids were busy living their best, delightful lives. To Emma's left, a small gang appeared to be Going On A Bear Hunt; to her right, a trio used toy cars as paintbrushes on a large sheet of paper. On the far side of the garden, the mud kitchen was proving as popular as ever, while coming towards them were two boys, each holding a piece of string and giggling hysterically. Attached to the pieces of string were small tree branches.

Emma raised her eyebrow, and Laura turned to follow her gaze. She laughed.

"Ah, dog logs. We played that game in Forest School on Monday and those two have been obsessed ever since!"

"Very cute," Emma said.

"Sorry, the spots," said Laura. "Well, I noticed them first on Archie."

"Archie Hopkinson?" asked Emma, almost without thinking.

"No, Archie Andrews," Laura replied, also without thought—the running joke of the two Archies had simply become part of the Happy Woodland vernacular—"although I did find them on Archie Hopkinson later. Anyway, not long after I saw them, Matt found some on Sammie, Lola, and Lily; Kirsty saw them on Aubrey and Zach; and then Margot found some on George, Millie, and Joseph. That's everyone who's in today."

"Strange," said Emma, barely aware she'd spoken the word out loud.

"Really strange," Laura agreed, "but, as I said to Clara, none of the kids have a fever. All their nappies and toilet doings are normal and, as you can see, they're as lively as ever."

Laura flung her arms out to indicate the normal maelstrom of Badger Sett fun that was going on around them. Unfortunately, it was right at the same time that one of the dog log-toting children was walking past. Laura's hand caught him across the side of the head, which was covered in a delightful, hand-knitted rainbow woolly hat, and the little chap flopped to the leaf-covered ground.

"Oh, Aubrey!" Laura turned bright red. "I'm so sorry, little one! Let me help you up."

It was only then Emma realised how quiet the garden had become. Seconds ago, the air had been filled with the sound of toddlers having a great time. But now, nothing. It was as close to silent as being outside could get—and not just here in the Badger Sett garden. It seemed as though every child on the premises had been muted.

The fallen child—Aubrey—was trying to get onto his hands and knees, adding a fresh layer of mud to his already-filthy jumpsuit in the process. Emma also bent towards him to help set him back on his feet, but not before glancing to her side.

They were being watched. The children had all stopped and were staring at Laura and her. The eyes of every child in the Badger Sett garden were on her, and even though she couldn't see them, she knew all of the other children across the whole site right now were doing the same.

Emma saw this, but didn't really take it in, as her instinct was still to help pick Aubrey up. Only once he was back on his feet and holding the string attached to his dog log did Emma realise the eeriness of that scene.

She snapped her head up and looked around.

No one was looking at her. The garden was as it always was: full of life, with the volume cranked accordingly. The mud kitchen, the Bear Hunt, the painting cars ... they were all in full swing. None of the other staff had seemed to notice what she had.

Laura stood up and dusted her hands on her trousers as Aubrey and his pal continued on their dog log walk.

"I really should have learned to not talk with my arms by now!" she said.

Both women laughed.

"What do you think, then, about these spots?"

"They're weird, but I don't think they're dangerous. Just make sure you tell every parent about them at pick up later, explain that they're otherwise fine, and ask them to keep an eye on them."

"OK." Laura smiled. "Thanks for coming out in the cold to see us. I feel like I've wasted your time a bit."

Emma shook her head. "Not at all. That's what I'm here for. You did the right thing. Call me if anything changes."

"Will do. Thanks again, Emma."

Laura jogged after Aubrey, obviously still feeling awful about knocking the little guy over despite him having long-since moved on, as toddlers do. Emma took one final look around the garden. She still felt like she was being watched, but as her eyes struggled to keep up with everything that was going on in front, she told herself she was being silly—that she'd imagined what had happened a few moments earlier.

And she probably *had* been watched. Any time a Grown Up from the office came outside, it was a big event—a spectator sport, in fact—and the kids would usually gawk at the strange-but-familiar visitor.

She left the Badger Sett garden and headed back to the office, not forgetting to stop in with the preschoolers and to see all of those Very Important Things they had to share with her. And they were, indeed, Very Important ... depending on your definition of important of course.

***

Nothing of note happened for the next hour and a half.

***

Mid-afternoon, Happy Woodland Nursery main office

This time, it was Emma who answered the office phone.

"Happy Woodland Nursery," she answered. "Emma speaking."

"Hi, Emma. It's Matt, over in the Badger Sett,"

said the voice at the other end. "Laura asked me to give you an update on the spots situation."

"Oh, yes. What's going on with them?"

"Well, the spots are all still there, but everything else is fine. No fevers, no unusual behaviour. Nothing bad at all really."

"Did lunch go OK?" asked Emma.

"Yep. They had cheesy pasta—popular as ever! In fact ..." he paused.

"Go on, Matt," Emma said.

"Well, that was something slightly different," he continued. "I've never seen them so hungry, every single one of them. They were ravenous—we actually ran out of food!"

Emma let out a small laugh. "Oh wow. Bet that was unpopular."

"Now that you mention it, they did all go quiet when I explained they'd eaten everything. They all stared at me at the same time, like they were genuinely angry with me."

Emma's stomach was suddenly full of butterflies. Her face lost some of its colour and she became aware of her heartbeat in her ears. She was instantly back in the garden that morning, feeling the combined burning gaze of every child on site.

"At least, it felt like that." Matt's voice snapped Emma back to the present. "But I probably imagined it. It's just that they usually *never* stop talking when they're 'round the table."

Emma felt the knot in her core slowly unravel and she let out the breath she didn't know she was holding.

"Anyway, that's all I have to add. Margot and Kirsty are just getting the last few down for their naps."

"OK. Thanks for the update, Matt. If you can have someone from the room check in towards the end of the day with another, that would be really helpful. Have a fun afternoon."

It was only after she'd hung up that Emma noticed the dark—almost black—spiral she'd carved into her notebook with a pencil that she didn't realise she'd been holding. Round and round and round until, at some point unknown to her, the stick of graphite had snapped—actually snapped —in half. There were splinters in Emma's palm and even a few drops of blood, but she hadn't even felt it.

Why am I so worried? she thought. *Everything is fine, so why have I snapped a pencil in half?*

Emma stared at the broken writing implement and the doom-filled black spiral she'd scrawled for a moment, then shook her head. It was fine. Everything was fine.

She took herself off to the kitchen to microwave her can of tomato soup.

***

Naptime, Badger Sett room

As Matt hung up the phone, Kirsty and Margot tidied the line of debris left abandoned by the now-sleeping toddlers in the corner of the room. Cuddly toys, model cars, wooden kitchen utensils, even a rogue glove—it was like a two-year-old had taken over an episode of *The Generation Game*, or at least been given the task of choosing that week's prizes.

While Kirsty carried an armful of stuff over to the toy box, Margot bent over to pick up a book. As she did, she caught a reflection of something strange in the plastic storage boxes mounted to the wall out of the corner of her eye.

It looked as though all of the children were sitting bolt upright, staring at her.

She half-jumped and quickly looked away from the reflection towards the kids.

They were asleep. All of them.

Margot shook her head and grabbed the book, only to subsequently drop the three *Hey Duggee* figures she was holding in her other hand.

Sighing, she scrabbled over to grab them from where they'd landed near the full-length mirror the team had installed so the children could enjoy pulling faces at themselves. Margot glanced in the mirror and properly jumped this time.

Again, the children were all sat bolt upright, staring at her with looks of pure hatred and fury.

Trying to keep her breathing steady, she slowly turned back to the room. No children staring at her. They were all still sleeping. Was she imagining it?

Margot dumped the toys in their box and hurried back to the rest of the staff, still holding the discarded book.

Kirsty, Matt, and Laura were making cups of tea when they saw Margot's expression. All of them felt their pulse quicken.

"What's wrong, Margot?" asked Laura.

Before she could answer, things started happening.

The drawers in the small kitchen area of the Badger Sett flew open, then slammed shut one at a time, while the kids' coats and bags rattled so hard on their colourful pegs that they spilled onto the floor.

"What on earth—" began Kirsty, when the two doors to the Sett—the main entrance and the emergency exit—locked from the inside with a defiant and definite *click*.

The staff looked at each other, then turned to the nap area to check on the children.

They were no longer asleep.

Every child's eyes were open, and they were slowly getting to their feet.

First Sammie, then Lola, then Lily.

Next was Aubrey.

Archie Andrews and Archie Hopkinson stood up together, Zach following immediately after.

George, Millie, and Josh did the same behind this group, but they were blocked from view.

None of the children smiled, none of them talked; none of them even blinked.

Once they were all on their feet, they started walking towards the staff. As they did, they linked hands, forming a circle around the adults, still looking like they were in some shared sleepwalking trance.

Just as Laura was about to say something to the children, they all formed a perfect O shape with their mouths. Then, the singing started. Only it wasn't singing, not really.

It was *broadcasting*. Those little mouths were like a circle of tiny speakers all tuned to the same frequency.

"Ring-a-ring-a-roses," the children chanted and started to skip around the adults in perfect time with each other, with the kind of grace and balance normal two-year-olds don't possess, "a pocketful of posies. Atishoo, atishoo, we all ... fall ..."

The children stopped skipping.

"... downnnnnnnnnnnnnnnnnnnnnn," they finished, holding the final note for an unnaturally long time.

Rather than cut the sound off, that final consonant seemed to break up, like a radio losing signal, morphing into white noise—loud, ear-splitting white noise.

The adults instinctively huddled closer to each other for protection from the circle of hissing toddlers. The children took a step towards them, still making that awful sound.

Another step. Laura noticed that one of the Archies was holding the phone, but she was too terrified to even work out which Archie it was.

The children took another step together. As they did, their eyes all started glowing a revolting, toxic bright yellow.

They took another step towards the adults and the volume of the white noise coming from their mouths ramped up several notches. That's when the grown-ups started to scream. They looked around in a blind panic for a way out, but there was none. The circle was complete, the children coming closer—each with their mouths open, their eyes glowing, and two small, perfectly circular spots somewhere on their face, now more prominent than they'd been all day.

The spots looked alive.

Kirsty noticed Archie holding the phone— Archie Hopkinson, as it happened—laughing into it, before pushing the big red button to cut off whoever was on the other line. She felt scared adult hands grabbing hers and pressed herself against the rest of her colleagues in the middle of the menacing circle.

A circle that was closing in.

The white noise was excruciating, the adults screaming themselves hoarse and then, the room bleached out in a bright, white light.

All the noise, all the horror, was lost in the glow.

***

Home time, Happy Woodland Nursery car park

Paul yanked the strap on his son's car seat tight, securing him in place, and then swivelled him round to face the iPad that was mounted to the back of the passenger seat. The current hit video—that one of some Japanese guy pushing *Thomas the Tank Engine* toys down a ramp into a bucket of mud—was already playing and Aubrey locked onto it straight away.

"Let's go home, dude," Paul said, then shut the car door. As he walked around the back of the vehicle, dropping his son's nursery bag in the boot and then continuing round to the driver's door, he found himself chewing over the weirdness that had been tonight's pick-up.

First, Aubrey seemed quieter than usual. Then again, it was a Friday—a Friday after a long week—and today's good weather would have undoubtedly been maximised by the nursery staff, with as much time spent running the garden as possible. *Probably just tired*, Paul thought.

Second, the staff appeared off-kilter too. Not just tired, but almost coming in and out of focus. Even during the course of the two-minute hand-over chat, Matt had seemed to lose the thread a couple of times—and Kirsty did the same with Archie Andrews' parents, from what Paul had overheard.

Still, he thought, *toddlers are exhausting. That's the big secret everyone keeps from you before you become a parent: how you come to dread weekends and how going back to work on a Monday is actually a chance to relax and recharge. They're probably just shattered, like I will be by Sunday afternoon.*

Paul pushed his key into the ignition and started the car. He flipped on the headlights to cut through the dark November afternoon and plugged his iPod back into the USB hub. That was the deal he'd struck with Aubrey for car journeys —videos in the back for the little dude, Daddy's music up front for Paul, so long as he didn't turn it up too loud. And yes, Paul still had an iPod. Streaming be damned, he liked owning his music, even if it was still digital.

The opening riff of *Swarm* by Palm Reader whirled around Paul as he pulled out of the car park, his mind still ticking over.

It was the weird conversation about the spots that sat the most uncomfortably with him.

Paul wasn't too concerned about the spots themselves; sure, he'd never seen such perfect circles on his son's face before, but Matt had assured him that Aubrey didn't have a fever and that, apart from those little dots, was his normal self. Paul had tried some cliché dad quip in response to this—*Uh-oh, still a cheeky monkey, then!*—but it coincided with one of those strange lapses from Matt, where he seemed to check out for a moment.

What was bugging Paul the most was how every child was now heading home with a pair of spots somewhere on their face. The nursery staff were clearly having the same conversation with all the parents, and it was probably nothing, but all the other kids Paul had seen at pick-up had the same subdued vibe that his own small person did.

And, now he thought of it, hadn't Paul noticed two perfectly circular spots on Matt's face as they were talking? And on Kirsty's too?

Forget it, Paul thought as he signalled left and made the most of a gap in traffic by joining the main road and easing all the way up to fifth gear. *They're all just tired. It's that time of year—Christmas is in sight, but still a few weeks left to get through before we get a break.*

They're just tired, he thought again as *Swarm* gave way to the hypnotic, lumbering riff of *Internal Winter* that always calmed Paul right down.

In the back seat, Aubrey was staring at the video on the mounted iPad, but he wasn't watching it.

He was perfectly still, waiting. Then, as if responding to some silent cue, his mouth dropped into a perfect O. He started to make a strange crackling sound, like white noise.

The sound from Aubrey's mouth grew louder, loud enough to seep into Paul's music. Paul frowned at the interference and tried jiggling the cable that connected his iPod to the car stereo, while also keeping his eyes on the road ahead.

As the noise got louder, Aubrey's eyes started glowing bright yellow. They reflected off the slightly-tilted iPad screen and onto the ceiling of the car—two throbbing yellow spots.

The car cruised towards a crossroads, and as it did, Aubrey turned his glowing gaze towards his father.

The Gift

'Twas the night before Christmas and all through the house, one creature was stirring. It wasn't a mouse, though—the thing scurrying about was a mild-mannered, likeable man in his thirties called Harris.

As had become his Christmas Eve tradition, Harris slipped out from under the covers and crept downstairs to the back door without pausing to take in just how darned festive he and Sam had made the place look for the next day. The tree was stunning—Sam's idea to apply a gold-and-white colour scheme really made it look classy—while the fireplace was framed with real holly leaves taken from Harris's mum's garden, and the twinkly little lights Sam had woven into them were just excellent.

It didn't end there; everywhere else in the house you looked shouted FESTIVE! Streamers, paper chains, mistletoe, Christmas cards, even home-made bunting with a sleigh bell on every fourth triangle. Sam had outdone themselves this year and they were rightly proud, but at this moment, Harris had only one thing on his mind: something he was expecting to be outside.

He flicked on the patio light and, sure enough, it was sitting there—waiting for him.

The gift.

For the last ten years, the oddest thing had happened to Harris on Christmas Eve. At some point between 10pm and whatever stupid time it was now, someone left him a gift on the patio.

From the outside, it looked the same every year: a cube about a foot long in each direction wrapped in festive metallic red paper that was dappled with flecks of green and a lid that you could remove but only by squeezing your hands against the side of it and letting the bottom of the box slowly slip down from its top. The whole package was finished off with a thick gold ribbon and a crisp white tag bearing his name and the current year, written in roman numerals, in beautiful gold calligraphy at the bottom right corner of the lid.

It was almost too perfect-looking, like the kind of Christmas present a child would draw, but that made it even more appealing to Harris. It had the Christmas magic that fills you up as a young child, that gets shoved into a corner of your mind somewhere as a teenager, but which ultimately never really goes away.

Harris had no idea where or who the gifts came from, but they had quietly become the highlight of his year, every year.

When the first one appeared a decade ago and Harris spotted it as he was locking up, he assumed it had been a cute offering from his then-new wife, who was already tucked up in bed at that point—perhaps as a way of marking their first Christmas together as a married duo.

But when he opened that first gift, tugging the ribbon so the knot gave way and the gold material flopped onto the ground, then slowly edging the lid off and trying his best not to tear the impressive wrapping paper, he realised Sam had had nothing to do with it. Inside that box ten years ago was an advert for a job with the words 'next step' written on it. It was a job Harris could do—a step up, sure, but he was qualified enough. It was simply something he would have never considered, not at that stage in his career.

Harris had applied for that job and, well, got it—his first managerial role and a seat at all the important meetings in a capacity that wasn't simply note-taking. His new role suddenly gave him a professional voice, and it turned out to be hugely important; that promotion ten years ago was the first of four in quick succession, and he was now at the point in his career where he was, effectively, set for life. There was only one more promotion left for him to achieve, but he had no desire to be CEO any time soon. With the money he was on now, he could do another ten years and then take ludicrously early retirement. He couldn't wait, and it was all down to that first gift from his unknown supporter.

More Christmases came—every year, as it happened—and more gifts came with them.

Harris soon got the sense that his special Christmas Eve delivery was actually coming from a future version of himself. It sounded crazy without the context behind it, but the more Harris thought about it, the more it seemed logical—no one else could know his life so intimately to the point where the contents of that beautiful gift box were always something he needed, even if Harris didn't know it at the time.

Each year brought a nudge towards something that would benefit Harris and, by extension, Sam: the betting slip with Leicester City's name on it eight months before they embarked on their 1,000–1 title-winning season, the hand-drawn map to the spot in the park in Kingsworth where he found an abandoned dog that would soon be joyfully adopted by Harris and Sam, or even the creepy one—the page of a calendar with STAY HOME scrawled on the 19th of June, a day that saw Harris's usual commuter train derailed at high speed just outside Foolsden with devastating consequences—hundreds died, hundreds more were terribly injured, yet Harris survived. And he did it simply by trusting the gift.

Those boxes had earned Harris's trust, and he repaid that trust by never telling a soul, not even Sam.

That had been the hardest part, because apart from the annual gift, he and Sam shared everything with each other. They were a team: they talked, they conferred, and they grew together. Harris had desperately, desperately, *desperately* wanted to tell them about it, but some part of his brain knew the importance of keeping quiet and so he followed his own advice. After a while, it became kind of easy—he simply had to make sure they were home every Christmas Eve. That had been a doddle during the pandemic, but that time a few years earlier when Sam had suggested the whole family decamp to a hotel in the Lake District had been tricky to negotiate. If ever they'd come close to a proper, full-on disagreement, it had been then.

In the end, Harris had come with a genuinely convincing plea that Christmas Eve: at home, just the two of them, was his most favourite part of the whole festive period. From the Big Day through to New Year, they were barely at home, rushing as they did from family member to family member; Harris and Sam both being children of divorced parents meant lots of places to visit. With all that travelling, hunkering down in cramped guest rooms or on lumpy sofa beds, they hardly got any quality time together. Christmas Eve at home was their only chance.

And so, much to Harris's relief, the 24th became *their* day and night, and the family respected —and sort of adored—it. Of course, it also made it super-easy for Harris to open the gift each year, which is why he had left the warmth of his marital bed just a few minutes ago, now feeling the way he did as a kid at this time of year.

He gently turned the key in the back door, pushed the handle, and slipped outside. His heart beat wildly as he approached the box. With all the secrecy involved—self-imposed, sure, but still there —this yearly ritual almost had a seedy quality to it. It felt *naughty*, which is probably why it was even more exciting with each year that passed.

Harris leaned forwards and grabbed the beautiful present, then tucked it under one arm and bunched his dressing gown in his left hand so he could sit on one of the patio chairs. Lost in the spectre of the gift, he barely felt the cold wood seeping through his pyjama trousers and boxer shorts to his buttocks and the back of his thighs underneath.

The gift was not only capable of warming his heart—it fired up his entire soul.

Wondering what might be in it this year, Harris

set his favourite routine of the year in motion. He patiently, slowly untied the ribbon, the impossibly smooth feel of it under his fingertips so calming it was almost sensual. Just touching the ribbon alone was worth getting out of bed for; it felt expensive, luxurious, and special.

Once the ribbon was untied and had dropped away from the box, Harris set it aside, then grabbed the lid with both hands and held the box an inch or so above his lap. He slowly squeezed the lid as the box slipped down—gently, gently, gently—until it came free.

The gift was open for another year. Harris's heart thudded with a renewed intensity—the excitement never lessened, not even after ten years of this personal bit of Christmas magic—and he ached to know what the latest gift had to offer him and Sam.

Harris peered inside.

And frowned.

He reached into the box, took out a small package wrapped in green tissue paper, then absent-mindedly pushed the empty box off his lap and down to the ground below his slippered feet.

A gift *within* the gift. That wasn't normal.

Heck, none of this was, but usually, the gift was just *there*. Take the lid off and, boom, there it was —no further searching or opening needed.

Perhaps it's a tenth anniversary special edition, Harris thought.

He tore off the tissue paper and sat for a moment staring at what it had been hiding.

There were two things: a digital stopwatch and what looked like the back of a playing cards.

The stopwatch was running, counting backwards with a delicate *bip-bip-bip* to mark each second. It had just under a minute to go.

Curious, Harris thought and was lost for a few beats, woolgathering. Then he turned the card over.

It wasn't a playing card.

It was a Tarot card. Death, to be precise.

For a moment, Harris didn't react. Then he panicked. He threw the card onto the patio like it was on fire and grabbed the stopwatch again, squinting at its display. Once his brain registered what his eyes were telling him, he jolted; he saw there were just five seconds left.

Harris jumped to his feet just as the watch beeped, signalling its countdown was almost over.

What the hell was going on here? This wasn't how things worked with the gift! Unless the last ten years had all been a game—an incredibly long one —to win his trust before, bang!—thank you and goodnight, Harris.

As the stopwatch flicked from two, to one, to zero, his face scrunched up—contorted with tension—and he waited, holding his breath.

Beep-beep! Beep-beep! Beep-beep!

Nothing happened.

Stupid, Harris thought, *just future me keeping me on my toes.* He sat back on the patio chair and let out a huge sigh as the thing creaked under his full weight sinking back into it. He leaned back, stretching his legs out straight, and placed his heels on the ground, trying to release as much tension from his body as possible.

He took a calming breath—in for the count of four, out for the count of eight—which helped. He took another and focused on nothing other than the stars. They were looking pretty spectacular tonight, given how clear of clouds the sky was.

When he felt calm again, Harris allowed himself to start chewing this one over. This was certainly the most bizarre, the most alarming and, frankly, the most disappointing gift he'd received yet. Was it significant? Were his gifts changing from this point onwards? Was the magic—the real, life-changing magic—finally moving onto someone else, someone who needed it more?

Quickly becoming lost while pondering all this, Harris failed to notice the slight breeze of something moving swiftly past him, or the sound of his back door being locked from the inside, or the shadow moving away from the door and towards the stairs, or the other thing that was stuck in the tissue paper.

Instead, he gave in to that feeling of festive satisfaction and drifted off. As he did, the tissue paper with its final hidden item slipped from his hand and tumbled to the ground, turning end-over-end, becoming separated from its tissue case. It landed face up next to the discarded Tarot Card and now-dead stopwatch. This previously hidden item would be the first thing Harris saw when he eventually woke up and finally put all of the clues together. But, by then it would all be too late. Yet for now, as Harris dozed under the stars in the soft comfort of his favourite dressing gown, there it lay between his slippered feet, staring up at him, the final piece of the puzzle all ready for him to wake up.

Time's up, death, and...a photo of Sam.

Once More Round
the Sun

The year was almost done, which meant she was running out of time.

Auld Lang Syne was mere moments away and she still hadn't found anyone suitable. She wasn't panicking yet—this very same club had served her well a year ago after all—but knew she needed to get a move on.

The past three hundred and sixty-four days had been good—plentiful, in fact. She'd fed well, had control throughout, and had simply enjoyed herself; she'd almost been sad to dispose of him earlier today.

Almost.

But she hadn't survived this long by being sentimental. She'd made it this far with smart choices, ones made in the few minutes that ended one year before starting the next.

All of which meant she had about three minutes —five at the max—to find next year's host. Again, panic wasn't on her agenda, but she was anxious.

She looked around the room again, letting her eyes land on every one of the males present who didn't appear to be with any type of partner, her mind making a snap judgement as to their suitability. That mind was well-versed in this scenario so she allowed it to do its thing.

No.

No.

Nope.

Maybe?

No.

Definitely not!

Perhaps.

Possible.

No.

Then, just as she always did, she found one. In fact, he'd been one she'd marked earlier in the night and had forgotten about. She should have trusted that instinct there and then, because he ticked every box: single, healthy, the right age, and—most importantly—drunk.

Very drunk, as it happened.

Even better, she noticed, he'd become separated from his friends. It was perfect timing—there was enough of the year left for one more song and then the countdown would begin, followed by the weird arm-in-arm swaying these humans insisted on doing every New Year's Eve, before moving onto the real fun.

The feeding.

She moved effortlessly across the dance floor towards him, touched his wrist, and smiled beautifully when his diluted eyes met hers. She leaned in close and whispered something in his ear. He smiled, nodding, then followed her towards the quickly-forming circle of revellers, stumbling slightly as the previous five hours of drinking caught up to him.

She knew that when human males looked at her, they saw a pair of beautiful eyes, a perfect smile and full, kissable lips. They always wanted her, just like this year's pick wanted her—she could see it in his eyes. When she looked at a human male in just the right way, she was irresistible, regardless of how many drinks had set up diversions on the high-ways between the eyes, the brain, and loins. When a human male was *this* drunk—and separated long enough from their friends to stop even caring—it wasn't even like hunting at all. *Fish in a barrel* was the human idiom she thought worked well for this situation.

The song ended and the countdown began. Time for another year, another project.

She took a deep breath, enjoying the festivities, the camaraderie, the anticipation. Yes, this year had been good. But looking into the eyes of her latest project, *next* year was going to be even better.

Should auld acquaintance be forgot, and never brought to mind?

Happy
New
Year!
DM '24

Start As You Mean To Go On

Fittingly, this is the story that was the genesis for the entire collection. It was the first one I wrote and it gave me the idea of setting one story in each month of the year. My first draft of this was written on New Year's Day in 2021. That year, I'd set myself a resolution of simply writing for 15 minutes every day. By the time 2022 burst through the door, I had 365 very short stories—many of which I used as starting points to turn into something longer. With this one, I added more build and more dread —then made it hornier in my second run-through of this collection because, well, why not?

Content warning: kidnapping, implied torture/mutilation

The Strange Phenomenon of Epping Manor

This was written for an anthology call themed around either haunted or missing houses—I forget which now. Anyway, my tale got rejected but I liked it enough to tweak it a little more and then include it here. I've since drafted a novel featuring the police officers we meet here—hopefully you'll get to read that story soon!

Content warning: missing person, ghosts

You're Melting

Another story that was initially written for an open anthology call—this time the request was for stories set in a graveyard. I loved writing this one and would say it's the best story I've written. So, to see it rejected from the initial call but also for at least another five since was hard to take. However, I never lost faith in it and knew it would have a place here. Someone's yuck is always someone else's yum!

You're Melting first appeared in *Tiny Tales of Terror, Volume 4: You're Melting and other stories* (ISBN 979-8870279510), published by Dave Musson on 29 November 2023.

Content warning: extreme gore, rats

Time Capsule

This one started life as one of my 15-minute pieces in 2021. I found a prompt online that suggested writing a story based around a time capsule being opened. So, that's what I did…and it got weird.

Mirrored

This story is very special to me; it was the first piece of fiction I ever had published. I wrote it specifically for the anthology that it appeared in—a collection of circus horror stories—and it all came out in a couple of hours where I properly lost myself in the tale and let it pour out. Oh, and if you think you don't know the song mentioned in this one then Google it, I'm certain you will recognise it.

Mirrored first appeared in *Welcome to the Funhouse: A Horror Anthology* (ISBN 978-1919613208), published by Blood Rites Horror on 29 June 2021.

Content warning: suicidal ideation, violence, bullying

Litha

In what is something of a running theme, this was another that I wrote for a specific anthology call and that didn't make the cut. Litha was created for a collection of religious horror stories—obviously, I embraced the pagan/culty side of things. This was a blast to research traditional summer solstice activities and then weave them into a very British story. Also, making Boomers the villains? That was pretty fun too.

Litha first appeared in *Tiny Tales of Terror, Volume 3: Litha and other stories* (ISBN 979-8398248937), published by Dave Musson on 15 June 2023.

Content warning: extreme violence and gore

Anchor

Another that started life as a 15-minute brain-dump. I'd used a random word generator to give me a prompt for that day's writing and it spewed out 'paperclip'. Everything then just fell into place pretty easily.

Anchor first appeared in *The Reach* Literary Magazine, published Summer 2022. It also later appeared in *Tiny Tales of Terror, Volume 2: Anchor and other stories* (ISBN 979-8398245967), published by Dave Musson on 5 May 2023.

In Too Deep

This story was originally written and accepted for an anthology of deep sea horror stories. However, the publisher of that collection ceased to exist and so my little story was homeless. Fast forward a couple of years and a couple more rejections later and it got picked up and unleashed on the world. At the time of writing the first draft I'd just finished rewatching the entire *Final Destination* franchise. I think the influence of those films here is pretty obvious!

In Too Deep first appeared in *HorrorScope: A Zodiac Anthology: Volume 3* (ISBN 979-8398626513), published by H. Everend on 5 September 2023.

Content warning: sharks, gore, open water

Here's Lookin' At You

Old paintings can be creepy, right? The way their eyes follow you round the room—nope, not for me thanks. Anyway, I knew I wanted to do something with that as an idea but struggled to unlock it. Then, I watched the movie *Men* and the scene where an entire tree's worth of apples fell to the ground proved to be the spark I needed, and everything flowed from there.

Content warning: locked doors/claustrophobia

Halloween Special - The Hunt For Rupi-K

This was one of the most fun to write. I wanted to put together a slasher and I wanted you to be glad when each victim snuffed it. The unlikeable lads here all take their names from a list of most hated YouTubers that I found online...I thought that just worked, you know? This story was actually accepted for a Halloween-themed anthology, but sadly that collection never ended up being born.

Content warning: extreme violence and gore

Spots

If a movie ever gets made of this story, the director would legitimately be allowed to say it was 'based on actual events'. One afternoon, I collected my son from nursery and he had a couple of small spots on his face—as did lots of his classmates. He was fine, and they went away pretty quickly, but it sent something spinning in my grey matter. Also, I got to have a character listen to my favourite band, Palm Reader—I advise you to do the same, they are wonderful and I'm still not ok that, by the time you read this, they will have split up.

Spots first appeared in *Eidolotry #3*, published by Psychotoxin Press on 1 January 2023. It later appeared in *Tiny Tales of Terror, Volume 1: Spots and other stories* (ISBN 979-8398244311), published by Dave Musson on 5 May 2023.

Content warning: creepy kids

The Gift

Another that started life with a 15-minute version. I was feeling both Christmassy and spooky, and wanted something that felt wholesome for most of its duration before giving you a stinger at the end.

The Gift first appeared in *Christmas of the Dead, Yule Cate Codex* (ISBN 978-81-968227-2-9), published by Wicked Shadow Press on 20 December 2023.

Content warning: implied murder

Once More Round the Sun

You probably won't be surprised to know I wrote this on New Year's Eve in 2021, my final 15-minute tale. I realised in about October that it might be fun to catch up with whoever or whatever it was we met at the start of the year, and so ended up starting the cycle all over again. Ka is after a wheel after all.

Dave Musson is a glasses-wearing, bearded human being from the middle of England who likes heavy music with loud guitars, watching movies, and reading creepy stories. He has more hobbies than he should really have time for; playing in a band, hosting a bunch of podcasts, writing, and running a Stephen King-themed YouTube channel.

Dave lives at home with his wife, sons, and annoying dog - he made his debut as a published fiction writer in 2021's *Welcome to the Funhouse*, from Blood Rites. He was also a finalist in the Bellingham Review's 2022 Tobias Wolff Prize for Fiction, and has been published on *The Horror Tree*, and in *Psychotoxin Press* and *The Reach* Literary magazine.

Subscribe to Dave's newsletter and get a free mini collection of short stories: davemussonauthor.com/newsletter

Follow Dave on Instagram instagram.com/davemusson

Find Dave talking about Stephen King on YouTube youtube.com/@DaveReadsKing

ACKNOWLEDGEMENTS

Thanks to Rooster Republic Press for the fantastic cover art.

I've been fortunate to have two brilliant women edit this collection for me, both spotting silly typos of mine, tightening my writing, and offering suggestions that really elevated these tales. So, thanks to Kelly Brocklehurst for pushing me to flex my horror muscles on the first draft, and to Diana Salazar for making those muscles scream with a terrible, awful pain on the final run through! Any remaining errors are on me.

Massive high five to Jamie Stewart, Jason Pellegrini, Garth Jones, Thomas Gloom, Spencer Hamilton, and Caitlin Marceau for offering such kind words that I've been able to use to help promote the collection. They are all incredible writers and I urge you to check out their work. I'm truly very lucky to have their endorsement.

Thanks to everyone on my mailing list for the constant support, my subscribers on YouTube and followers on Instagram. Most of all, thanks to *you* for giving this collection a chance!

One of the best ways in which you can support indie authors—aside from buying their books of course - is to leave a rating and review on places like Amazon once you've finished reading it. Seriously, they're super helpful and super important—and the positive ones help massage the fragile egos of me and my fellow authors.

Even a one sentence review can make a huge difference, so I'd be really grateful if you could spare a few moments to rate and review this book you've just finished on either Amazon or Goodreads—or, even better, on both!